The Secret Life of Thomas Bradford

For Samantha

Best Wishes
Anne Knoll

With LVE
Thomas B.

Anne Knoll

Royal Fireworks Press

Unionville, New York
Toronto, Ontario

For my grandchildren, Jessica, Bryan, Kyle, Kevin and Jordan

'Tis only noble to be good,
Kind hearts are more than coronets.

Alfred Lord Tennyson

Royal Fireworks Press
First Avenue, POB 399
Unionville, NY 10988-0399
(914) 726-4444
FAX: (914) 726-3824
email: rfpress@ny.frontiernet.net

Royal Fireworks Press
78 Biddeford Avenue
Downsview, Ontario
M3H 1K4 Canada
FAX: (416) 633-3010

ISBN: 0-88092-421-7

Printed on acid-free, recycled paper using vegetable-based inks in the United States of America by the Royal Fireworks Printing Company of Unionville, New York.

PROLOGUE

Thomas Bradford scampered to the top of the high wooden fence, looked down, looked back, closed his eyes and jumped. He landed on his feet, none the worse for wear, despite his wildly beating heart.

He looked around at the unfamiliar yard he now occupied. He dare not tarry long, for already excited voices could be heard on the other side of the fence:

"He's gone. Help. Find him, somebody."

"Do you see him?"

"No, he's not here. He must have jumped the fence."

Thomas didn't wait to hear more. There was an opening on the far side of the other fence, and he squeezed through it, catching the hated sweater on a nail and ripping it off his back.

Good, he thought. Now, if he could just manage to get the silly hat off, too, but he hadn't time for that now. They'd be after him, all of them, and they could run fast, faster even than Thomas, whose father had been famous for his cunning and speed.

But, they can't match me at climbing, he thought, looking up at the giant oak tree that loomed in his path. Digging his nails into the bark, he shinnied up the thick trunk. Higher and higher he climbed, until the branches grew weaker and he was afraid even his slight weight might pull them down.

1

Finding a sturdy branch, he straddled it, caught his breath and looked below. Now he felt like a human being, safe and superior as he peered down at the scurrying little figures of his tormentors.

They had formed a search party and were fanning themslves out over the area. *Let them look,* Thomas thought. He'd stay right here until dark if necessary, and then he was going on a search of his own. They'd never see him again, not any of them. Thomas was going to find his way home, back to his mother and all the dear people he'd loved and lost.

1

The Beginning

The very first thing that Thomas remembered was his mother. She was so beautiful and so good. When he snuggled close to her, and she sang to him in her beautiful, soft voice, he felt nothing in the world could ever hurt him. Of course, he had been a baby then, and life had been very simple. Thomas and his sisters had been content to do nothing but sleep and eat.

Soon though, Thomas became conscious of a world outside the comfort and security of the friendly dark. One morning his tightly shut eyes opened, and he looked around him. First he saw his mother, and she was just as beautiful as he had imagined her to be. Her eyes were sapphire blue. They stood out like jewels against her creamy whiteness. She was as graceful as a queen and indeed that is what they called her, those strange looking ones who came down to visit and whom Thomas later learned to love in spite of their ugliness.

Thomas's two sisters were dark like their father, while Thomas himself was just as white and beautiful as his mother. His nose and the tops of his ears were pale pink, as were his toes, but it was his eyes which were his most unique feature, for they did not match. One eye was blue, and the other was amber yellow. It was as though Thomas's mixed heritage proclaimed itself for all to see in the startling contrast of those eyes.

3

Queenie, Thomas's mother, was a pure-bred, white Siamese, a show cat with an ancestory reaching back through generations of prize-winning thoroughbreds. Thomas's father, on the other hand, was pure alley cat. He was nicknamed Tom by the Bradford family, who owned Queenie and who were plagued by the big tomcat's unwelcome visits to their yard.

They had tried everything short of murder to rid themselves of Tom. Charlie Bradford, husband of Dottie and father of Mark and Judy Bradford, threw sticks and stones at him, expertly aiming to avoid actually hitting Tom, but hoping to scare him. Dottie Bradford chased him from the yard daily with a broom, but it was all to no avail. As long as Queenie, occuping her favorite sunspot in the bay window, was visible from the outside, Tom would risk life and limb to gaze at her with adoring feline eyes.

It was twelve-year-old Mark Bradford who unwittingly played cupid for Queenie and Tom. Mark woke up one moonlit night to hear Tom yowling loudly in the yard. He padded downstairs half asleep, opened the kitchen door and threw a chicken leg out onto the patio.

"There, eat that and keep quiet," he called out officiously to the four-legged prowler.

The next morning the whole household was in an uproar. Queenie was missing. Judy Bradford, who was ten, was in tears. She was convinced catnappers had spirited her beloved Queenie away in the dark of the night.

"Nonsense," her father said. "The cat is hiding somewhere in the house."

"I've looked everywhere," Dottie Bradford told her husband quietly. "Could she have possibly gotten outside?"

4

"Nonsense," Charlie Bradford repeated. "That's impossible."

They all agreed vigorously that this was impossible, all except Mark, who agreed, but not quite so vigorously. He *had* opened the door to throw out the chicken leg, but he thought it wise not to mention the incident.

Coming events proved the wisdom of this decision, for several hours later Queenie turned up, very definitely on the outside. It was Mark who heard the familiar "Meow," though faintly, through the noisy sobs of his sister.

"Shut up your bawling. I think I hear her."

This news was so welcome that his sister did immediately stop crying, and even their mother forgot to scold Mark for saying, "shut up." Instead, she rushed to open the door, and there was Queenie, looking cool and calm and completely oblivious to the worry she had caused the Bradfords.

Later still, when it became obvious to Dottie that her prize show cat was about to produce some very unshowable half-breed kittens, Mark saw no reason to offer any explanation.

"I still can't imagine how Queenie got out," his mother would say over and over, and Mark would counter with, "What difference does it make? You said she could have one litter of kittens."

"I said a litter of Siamese kittens, Mark—not kittens like these will be."

"Aw, Mom. They'll be cute, and I already know lots of kids that'll be glad to take one."

"So do I," Judy said, eager to join the conversation. "Mary Agnes wants a girl kitten."

"Mary Agnes," Mark taunted. "We're not giving that dumb girl any of our kittens. Why doesn't she get a rabbit? She looks like one herself."

That said, he sucked in his lower lip, making his front teeth protrude in imitation of his sister's friend.

"Mary Agnes does not look like that," Judy protested, and their mother quickly changed the subject to restore peace.

The kittens were born in a wicker clothes basket, Queenie preferring that to the elaborate box the family had prepared for the birthing. She accomplished the feat alone, surprising the family one morning by appearing in the kitchen, slim and graceful once more.

"Queenie is skinny again," Judy shouted in disbelief and the whole family scrambled to the basement to confront an empty box.

"Where are the kittens?" the children asked.

"Don't worry. They're here somewhere," their mother assured them. "Sometimes cats want to choose their own place to have their kittens."

As if on cue, Queenie came downstairs. She marched right past the large wooden box, handcrafted for her by Charlie Bradford out of the lumberyard's best plywood, and cushioned with remnants of the softest material found in Dottie Bradford's sewing box. She headed for the laundry room and once there, hopped proudly into a large wicker clothes basket. Then, she said, "Meow," in a newly mature voice and glanced at the family, inviting them to view the new arrivals.

From the first, the whole family was completely taken with the kittens. Even Dottie Bradford, who had complained the most about the kittens' unsavory lineage, was won over.

"They're beautiful," she crooned, stroking Queenie, while the young mother purred in contentment and nursed her brood.

"Did I hear you right?" Charlie Bradford teased. "Tom, the derelict's kittens are beautiful?"

"Well they are," Dottie replied with a smile. "And, they're only half alley cat, you know. On their mother's side, they're pretty high-brow."

"High-brow or low-brow," Charlie answered, coming over and looking in the basket. "I'd say they're three handsome kittens, but seriously, Dot—what are we going to do with them? We can't keep four cats."

"I know that. When they're eight weeks old, I'll put an ad in the paper. We should have no trouble finding homes for them."

As the weeks passed, it became obvious to all the family that the little white male was the maverick of the litter. He was the first one to climb out of the basket, and he wore poor Queenie out picking him up and returning him, only to have him immediately climb out again. The Bradford children were amused by Queenie's attempts to discipline her wayward son. She would drag him by the scuff of the neck and then lift him off the floor and carry him in her mouth with his little feet dangling in the air. Then she would unceremoniously dump him on top of his sleeping sisters.

Soon all three kittens were leaving the basket, and Queenie no longer tried to keep them confined. They romped and played all over the basement. Thomas's sisters, whom Judy had temporarily named Mimi and Fifi, thought the Bradford basement was the whole of the world, but Thomas, named for his renegade father, thought differently.

7

He knew those impossibly high steps led somewhere, for he saw the humans and his own mother climb them and then disappear through the door at the top. Thomas was determined to find out what was up there.

2

Thomas Leaves Home

Thomas was tired. Climbing steps was hard work. He had only reached the fourth step and already his front legs ached from the effort of stretching, digging his claws into the treads and pulling up. Worst of all, his goal, the top, still looked far out of reach. How did his mother and the others get up there so fast? He sat quietly on the fourth step and thought about it.

The Bradfords only had two legs, but then they were such long legs (even Judy's and Mark's were long), so it was no problem for them. Thomas drew a mental picture of his mother climbing the steps, and suddenly the answer was clear to him. Nobody really climbed steps. The humans walked up, which was easy enough for them with their funny, long legs, but Thomas's mother actually jumped up the steps.

Thomas stood poised in the middle of the fourth step. He jumped and landed nicely on the fifth step. *This was going to be fun,* he thought—the sixth, the seventh. The top was getting closer and closer—the ninth, the tenth, and hurrah, he was at the top. Thomas was congratulating himself when the door opened and smacked him right in the face. Losing his balance, he somersaulted backwards. Down, down, down, he bounced, the ninth step, the eighth, the seventh...

"Oh, the kitten. Oh." It was one of the human's voices.

Suddenly strong, gentle hands picked him up. Thomas opened his eyes and saw that it was Judy who held him.

"Oh poor, poor Thomas, poor little kitty," she crooned, hugging him.

Thomas felt very secure, very happy and instinctively, without even knowing he was doing it, Thomas sang. He sang the way his mother had taught him, a soft, low song that went, "mmmmmmmmmmm."

Thomas had the soul of a Gypsy. Once he had mastered the stairs, there was no stopping him. He was all over the house—upstairs, downstairs, under beds, on beds, in and out of closets, and one day he leaped from the arm of a chair onto the window sill like he'd often seen his mother do.

Thomas peered through the glass to the great outdoors, and his little heart raced with excitement. Wonderous things met his gaze. He saw grass and trees, beautiful flowers, and in the yard next door, the strangest looking creature Thomas had ever seen. It was huge. It wasn't a human, for it had four legs and a tail. It certainly wasn't a cat—that he knew.

At the very moment that Thomas was poised at the window staring at the creature, it looked up at him. Then it made a horrible loud noise and raced around the yard like a crazy thing, jumping up on its hind legs and making that thunderous noise again. Thomas felt the fur on his tail stand straight up, and he arched his back. Later his mother told him that the creature was a dog and that it was a natural enemy to cats. Thomas, being his father's son, was more fascinated than fearful, and he decided that he would have to find a way to get outside and have a closer look at this thing called a dog.

Thomas's sisters did not share his love of danger and were content to play quietly on the floor with a ball of string or a paper bag. Queenie knew her little half-breed prince would not have it easy in the years to come, for Thomas was already at war with himself. He looked like a blue-blood, but the hot red blood of his father coursed through his veins.

After eight weeks, Dottie Bradford put an ad in the Sunday paper. It read: "Free to Good Homes—Part Siamese kittens, 1 male, 2 female, 1 white, 2 black."

Judy and Mark took the kittens outside to play on the cool grass. Now that the ad was in the paper, they knew it wouldn't be long before all the kittens would be gone. The children had known from the beginning that they couldn't keep them, but now that the time for parting was drawing near, they both made a last ditch effort to change their parents' minds. Judy cried and Mark had come up with every plausible excuse he could think of for why four cats would be better than one.

"Absolutely not," their father said, and they knew he meant it.

"If we could keep one," Judy began, but her brother cut her off.

"We can't, so why talk about it?"

"I know, but if we could. Which one would you want to keep?"

"Thomas," he answered without hesitation. "We already have one female cat and besides, I think Thomas is a cool cat. Look at him right now. He's not even afraid of old Jeff. Look—holy cow, he's slipping under the fence. Holy cow, he's going in old Jeff's yard."

"Oh Mark, get him," Judy cried. "Jeff might hurt him."

Thomas was nervous. Maybe he shouldn't have tried this, and he eyed the big dog with caution. One of the creature's paws was bigger than Thomas's head. The dog stared at Thomas, and Thomas stared right back. He felt the fur on his tail stand straight up. Thomas arched his back and started walking sideways in his excitement.

The creature crouched low, observing Thomas. Suddenly it started pawing the ground, and Thomas recognized the signal.

Thomas ran and the dog ran alongside of him. Judy screamed and Mark, who now straddled the fence, yelled at her, "Be quiet, dummy. They're playing."

Up and down the yard the two of them raced. Back and forth and faster and faster. Thomas was getting tired. He'd had enough of this game. Quickly sliding under the fence, he left the dog to chase himself up and down until he realized that the mysterious little visitor had vanished.

Mark and Judy laughed to see the puzzled expression on old Jeff's face. "You're a cool cat, Thomas," Mark said, and Judy picked Thomas up and hugged him.

Thomas licked her face with his little sandpaper tongue. He wasn't a lap cat like his sisters, but he didn't mind a little bit of cuddling now and then.

That night Queenie told her kittens the facts of life. They were eight weeks old, and it was time they were on their own. The family, she said, would find them all good homes and they must remember to conduct themselves always in ways that would make her proud of them. They must wash themselves at least ten times every day and always after eating. They must eat daintily and sparingly, never making a mess with their food or overeating like dogs.

That night Queenie slept in the box with them for the last time. Thomas's sisters slept as close to their mother as possible, luxuriating in the security of her soft, warm body, but Thomas, as always, slept a little to the side to show his independence. Queenie's deep blue eyes looked at him with love, and she stretched out her paw and encircled him. Thomas purred softly, and Queenie joined him in the age-old song of love and contentment.

Mimi was the first to leave, and she would only be moving around the corner. Judy's friend, Mary Agnes, took her the following day. Mimi was happy. Mary Agnes, despite Mark's low opinion of her, was a gentle girl, and she promised Judy she would take good care of the kitten.

Late that same afternoon, a tall man in a station wagon arrived at the house. He had called in the morning to inquire about the kittens. He told Dottie Bradford he wanted a pet for his little girl. It was her birthday and he wanted to surprise her with a kitten. Dottie would have preferred meeting the child, but the man assured her his daughter was a cat lover and would take good care of a kitten.

Dottie brought out Fifi and Thomas. The man seemed unable to decide between them until she mentioned that one was male and the other female.

"Oh, you'd better give me the male. My ex-wife wouldn't appreciate a female, I'm sure."

Dottie hesitated. "Are you sure a kitten will be..."

"It'll be alright. If it isn't, I can always bring it back, can't I?"

Dottie responded quickly. "Of course, and I really mean that, Mr. Martin. If for any reason your wife, er—your little girl's mother—doesn't want to keep the kitten, please bring it back."

"Sure," he said, and bending down, the man scooped Thomas up under his arm and carried him out to the car.

3

No Way To Treat A Prince

Thomas knew what an automobile was. He had watched them moving up and down the front street. The Bradfords had one, too, and Thomas had seen the family get in it and ride away, but he had never been in one himself.

This was a new adventure though, and it kept him from thinking about his mother and the Bradfords. He sat up on the back of the seat and looked straight ahead. He was a little anxious about being in the contraption, but he was determined to keep his dignity. He certainly wouldn't behave like the dogs he had observed riding in cars with their heads stuck out the windows, looking like fools.

It wasn't so bad, he decided. Turning corners was a little rough though, and he dug his claws in to keep from sliding.

"Ouch. Get off," the man yelled. The car jolted and Thomas dug in deeper.

CRASH—BOOM—BANG! Thomas had never heard such a racket.

He landed on the floor and when he picked himself up and looked out the window, there was a huge crowd of people gathered around the car. Mr. Martin was outside and he appeared to be arguing with a very distraught lady.

She said, "You drove right into my car. Are you crazy?"

"Madam, I'm sorry. I couldn't help it. I had a cat on my head."

15

"A cat on your head," the woman repeated.

Thomas dived back down on the floor. He was embarrassed and he didn't want anybody to see him. Looking around for a place to hide, he spied an opening and squeezed himself inside. He couldn't see anything because it was dark, but he could hear the voices outside clearly.

"Officer, this man ran right into my car. I was parked on the side..."

"Officer, I tried to explain to the lady it was an accident."

"No kiddin'," a voice from the crowd yelled.

Then another voice spoke up. "He said a cat was on his head. Ha, ha."

"Officer, let me explain. I have a kitten in the car. Here, I'll show you."

Thomas crouched down in the dark place. He didn't want Mr. Martin to find him.

"Well, where's this cat?"

"I don't know. It was here. It climbed on my head—that's why I lost control of the car."

"Tell it to the judge," a heckler offered.

Thomas didn't want to hear anymore. He just wanted to hide. Making himself as small as possible, he squeezed even farther back into a corner. He had no idea where he was, but it was a dark, dirty place. Wishing he was home with the Bradfords and his mother, he closed his eyes and tried to go to sleep.

Several minutes later, a loud noise jolted Thomas awake. It was so loud, it hurt his ears. Everything around him started to shake. There was nothing for Thomas to hold on to and he was slammed back and forth by a tremendous force.

Thomas was terrified. He was certain he would be killed and then his mother's voice came back to him.

"Remember you have nine lives to live. Don't squander them."

I won't, he promised himself. *If I get out of this, I'll make the other eight last a long time.* Another jolt, and Thomas felt his head crack. Then everything went black.

When Thomas woke up, he was in another strange place. Everything he saw was white—white walls, white floors and the man standing over him wore a white coat.

"He'll be alright," the man said. "But just to be on the safe side, we'll keep him overnight. He's had quite a shock, but the head wound isn't too bad."

"Is he healthy otherwise?"

This voice was familiar and Thomas saw that Mr. Martin was standing behind the man in white.

"Oh, he's a fine kitten," the stranger answered. "He's going to be odd-eyed though."

"Odd-eyed?" Mr. Martin repeated.

"Yes, it's a mutation. All kittens' eyes are blue at first. Then they turn to yellow at about nine weeks. Only the Persians and Siamese retain the blue color. This one will have one blue eye and one yellow eye."

The man held a light to Thomas's eye—"See the yellow starting to form in this eye," he said.

Mr. Martin looked and nodded his head. He really wasn't interested in Thomas's eyes. He was beginning to regret the whole idea of giving Courtney a kitten for her birthday. Already the cat had cost him plenty. The policeman had given him a ticket for reckless driving. He

17

would have to appear in court for that, and he expected to lose.

The damage to the other car should amount to a couple of hundred dollars, and his own car now sported a smashed headlight and several new dents which would have to be repaired. He wondered about the vet's fee, but it seemed a little mercenary to inquire about it now.

"Pick him up tomorrow morning," the man said and added with a smile, "Don't worry, he'll be fine. Cats are resilient animals. How did he get under the hood of your car anyway?"

Mr. Martin didn't feel like going into that. The whole thing had given him a splitting headache.

"Who knows?" he said wryly and walked out of the office.

Thomas was not overly fond of Mr. Martin, and he surmised the feeling was mutual, but after one night in the hospital, Thomas was glad to see a familiar face in the morning.

"He's as good as new," the doctor pronounced and handed Thomas over.

This time Thomas was put in a carrying case, and he didn't object. He was no more anxious than Mr. Martin to repeat yesterday's mistakes.

"Calamity Cat," Mr. Martin said as he placed the carrying case on the seat. "That's what you ought to be called." Then he laughed. "You should fit in well. Maybe you'll keep Gloria so busy she won't have time to badger me."

Thomas wondered who Gloria was. He soon found out though, for presently the car was stopped, the carrying case

18

was picked up, set down and Thomas knew by the smell that he was inside a house.

"Where's Courtney?" he heard Mr. Martin ask.

A female voice answered. "She's playing outside. You're late with my check, Harry."

"It's in the mail, Gloria."

"I need it, Harry."

"It's in the mail, Gloria."

"What's in that box?"

"Courtney's birthday present."

"You're late again. Her birthday was yesterday."

"I know that. It couldn't be helped. Just call Courtney, will you please?"

"Is there an animal in that box, Harry? You know I don't like dogs."

"It's not a dog."

"If it's a hamster, you can take it right out. Courtney's allergic to them."

"It's not a hamster, Gloria. It's a kitten. Now, will you please call Courtney?"

Thomas heard a door slam and then a high pitched voice screeched, "Daddy, you forgot my birthday."

"No, I didn't. I have it right here. Open the box."

Thomas wished he could just disappear and have them find the box empty. He didn't like the sound of them at all. They had rasping voices that hurt his ears, not like the Bradfords, whose voices were low and sort of musical.

"Oh, it's a kitten," Courtney squealed and she pulled Thomas roughly out of the box. "Look Mommy. It's all pink and white."

She was holding Thomas so tight he could hardly breathe.

"Put it down, Courtney. You're holding it too tight," her mother said. Then she turned to Mr. Martin. "What kind of cat is it?"

"An expensive one."

Gloria raised her eyebrows and looked sharply at Thomas. "It just looks like an ordinary cat to me."

"Well it's not. It's an unusual cat. The vet said so. It's an odd-eyed cat."

"I never heard of such a thing."

"It's got different color eyes," Courtney exclaimed, and Gloria peered closely at Thomas.

"Well, what do you know. Did you pay much for it, Harry?"

"Plenty," he answered and Gloria looked angry.

"I hope that doesn't mean my check..."

"Your check's in the mail, Gloria." Then he turned to his daughter and said, "What are you going to name it?"

"I'm going to call it Shirley."

"Shirley? That's a girl's name. It's a boy cat."

"I don't care. It looks like a girl, and that's what I'm calling it."

Thomas was furious. He looked at Courtney with disgust. *You can call me Shirley all you want,* he thought, *but I won't answer to it—ever.*

"Come on, Shirley," Courtney said and she picked Thomas up and held him tightly in her arms.

20

She took him outside to the yard where three of her girlfriends were waiting.

"Oh, what is that, Courtney?" one of the girls asked.

"It's a kitten, silly."

"Oh, let's see it. Where did you get it?" the third girl asked.

"My Daddy gave it to me for my birthday."

"Oh, isn't it cute? What's it's name?"

"Shirley."

"Can I hold it?"

"Just for a minute and hold it tight. I don't want it to get away."

Thomas was handed over to the other girl, and all three of them stared at him.

"Look, it's eyes are different colors," one said.

"Of course," Courtney answered importantly. "It's an odd-eyed cat, and it cost a lot of money. My daddy said so. Now hold it tight, and I'll be right back."

When Courtney was out of sight, the girl who held Thomas said, "She makes things up. I'll bet this kitten didn't cost a lot of money. Her father doesn't even have a lot of money. My father says Courtney's father's just a big bag of wind."

"Ssh, here she comes," the other one said.

Courtney was carrying a box and one of the girls asked, "What's that?"

"You'll see," Courtney answered, smiling mysteriously.

Thomas had a sneaking suspicion it had something to do with him and that he wasn't going to like it.

21

Courtney opened the box and the others said, "Oh, doll clothes!"

"These are from the doll I broke, and they should really look good on Shirley."

For a moment, Thomas had forgotten that he was supposed to be "Shirley." When the truth dawned on him, he made an heroic effort to escape, but it was too late. The other girl had already turned him over to Courtney, and she had him encased in her little steel fingers.

Thomas felt like a fool. They dressed him up in a pink sweater and bonnet. Courtney had wanted to get one of the dresses on him, but Thomas had ripped it with his back feet.

"Bad Shirley," Courtney said, smacking him on his head, which was still sore from the accident.

The bonnet, to Thomas's relief, kept slipping off until Courtney got the brilliant idea of punching holes in it for his ears to go through.

"Now, isn't Shirley adorable," she exclaimed, and the others all giggled and agreed.

Thomas's mind was made up. As soon as he got the chance, he was running away. What would his father say if he could see him now?

Queenie had told Thomas about his father. He had the largest territory of any cat in the neighborhood, and no cat dared challenge him. Big Tom was king of the alley and no mistake about it. Thomas had a tradition to uphold, and no little steel-fingered girl with a bag of wind for a father was going to stop him.

He pretended to be compliant, and Courtney said to the others, "I think Shirley likes being dressed up."

"Let's put Shirley in the baby carriage," one of the girls suggested.

Courtney threw the doll out of the carriage and thrust Thomas into its place. He let himself be tucked in and pretended to go to sleep. When Courtney walked behind the carriage to push it, Thomas jumped out.

♋   ♋   ♋

Thomas was amused, watching them from his perch high up in the tree. Courtney was crying and stamping her foot. "I want you to find him. I want Shirley back."

"Baby, we've looked everywhere. Daddy'll get you another cat."

"I don't want another cat. I want Shirley."

Courtney's mother spoke up then. "You don't seem so worried, Harry. I thought this cat cost you so much money."

"It did. It did, Gloria, but if Courtney wants another cat, I'll get her another cat."

"Well, big-time spender, my check better be..."

"Your check's in the mail, Gloria."

Courtney's girlfriends looked knowingly at one another and giggled.

Thomas closed his eyes. He'd take a nap and when he was positive they were gone, he'd come down. He had only one goal now, to find his way back home to the Bradfords. If they couldn't keep him, that would be OK. He'd join up with his father and become a street cat.

4

Vagabond Cat

It was almost dark when Thomas woke up from his nap. The Martins and Courtney's girlfriends had all disappeared, so Thomas cautiously climbed down the tree.

Going down was harder than going up, he discovered, but he kept remembering that his father was king of the alley cats, and he certainly wasn't going to be stuck up a tree.

Once on the ground, he was apprehensive, and he paused to get his bearings. It certainly wouldn't do for him to be captured now by walking right into one of their yards. Since he didn't know where the girlfriends lived, Thomas concluded it would be safer for him to take the front street.

The stupid doll's hat presented a problem there. He would surely be noticed walking down the street with a bonnet on his head. Knowing Courtney as he now did, he was certain, too, that she had blabbed about him all over the neighborhood, so the quicker he left the vicinity, the better, he thought.

Thomas pulled and tugged, but he simply could not get the thing off his head. Finally he decided to take his chances with it on. He judged the direction of the front street by following the sound of the automobile motors and once there, he made a beeline for the opposite side.

Several cars honked and he caught glimpses of startled looks on drivers' faces as they spotted him dashing across the street in his bonnet.

Once on the other side, Thomas felt safer. He had put a little distance at least between himself and Courtney Martin. He wouldn't feel really safe, though, until his sharp nose told him he was no longer in her neighborhood.

♋   ♋   ♋

Thomas had been running for a long time. It was now completely dark outside, and the October sky was dotted with bright stars and a full orange moon.

He stopped to rest under white marble steps. The neighborhood had subtly changed from residential to commercial, and although Thomas had no way of knowing it, he was in a rather sleazy part of town.

He was hungry and suddenly realized how long it had been since he had eaten. The meal at the animal hospital hadn't been the best, but he would gladly settle for more of the same at the moment. He sniffed the air and his keen sense of smell told him that somebody nearby was cooking.

Thomas followed his nose and it led him to a bar and restaurant around the corner. The door was open and a line of men sat on high stools at a long table. One of the men looked up as Thomas poked his head around the door, and Thomas quickly retreated behind a bush.

A few minutes later, two men emerged from the bar.

"What's your hurry," one said.

"I'm going home. I've had enough," the other answered.

"You only had two beers."

"Yeah, well I'm going on the wagon again. You heard about seeing pink elephants? Well, I won't even tell you what I just seen."

Thomas waited until they were out of sight, and then he scampered around to the back of the establishment. The Bradfords' kitchen had been in the back of the house. Maybe this one was, too.

The alley was dirty and littered with broken bottles and trash, but Thomas followed his nose and found the kitchen. Jumping up on the window sill, he looked inside. A man was in there slicing meat. He had on a white coat just like the doctor in the hospital had worn, and that alone was enough to make Thomas wary of him. On his head he wore a funny white hat, and in his hand, he held the biggest knife Thomas had ever seen. Thomas's stomach growled with hunger pangs as he watched the man lay the thick steaks on a platter.

He had to get in that kitchen, but how? The window was shut, and so was the door. Thomas thought about it. *What would my father do,* he wondered. He remembered his mother saying, "Your father was very clever. Being a street cat, he had learned to live by his wits and he knew how to use psychology on the humans. That's how he got me out of the house to meet him...."

That's it, Thomas thought. Of course, he didn't have his father's powerful voice, but there were other ways.

Thomas made several leaps against the garbage can before it finally fell over with a loud, tinny clatter. The door flew open, the cook ran out, and Thomas ran in. In two seconds Thomas was on the table, off the table and out the door with a big chunk of steak in his mouth.

"Hoodlums! I gife you Halloween. I cut you up in leetle pieces," the cook screamed, waving the knife at his phantom pranksters.

Thomas was two blocks away and already devouring his steak before the irate cook had returned to his kitchen to ponder the mystery.

Thomas felt better after he had eaten, but he was tired, and his little legs ached from running so long. He decided the alley was safer than the street, so he would spend the night here and get an early start in the morning. Climbing inside a giant hopper, he went to sleep.

Several hours later, a bottle was thrown into the hopper, landing on Thomas's paw and filling the container with a sickening odor. Thomas pushed it aside and settled himself again on the mound of paper which had become his bed. He had just gotten to sleep again when a second bottle flew into the hopper. The added smell was more than Thomas's delicate nose could take and he stuck his head outside for air.

He found himself looking squarely at the bottle thrower. The man was sitting on the ground and leaning against the wall. He had two more bottles of the same foul stuff beside him. He stared at Thomas and then quickly raised one of the bottles to his lips, taking a long swig. Thomas ducked back inside the hopper. His keen ears picked up the sound of approaching footsteps. Two more bottles landed in the hopper, and Thomas heard voices.

"Didn't I tell you to stay off my beat?"

"I ain't doin nothin', Ofsher."

"You're drinking in this alley."

"You see me with a bottle, Ofsher?"

"You just threw it in that hopper."

"I wouldn't look in there if I was you, Ofsher. There's a white cat wearin a pink bonnet in there."

"Sure there is, buddy. You just come along with me."

"But, Ofsher, there is a white..."

"What say we just leave her there. I'll tell ya, I seen a black cat around the corner, wearin a top hat and a tuxedo. Maybe they got a date, huh?"

The voices grew fainter, and Thomas went back to sleep. When he got up, he'd have to think of a way to get the ridiculous hat off his head.

CHAPTER

5

A Jungle Out There

Thomas had been wandering the city for a month. The bonnet, which had precipitated his decision to escape, was long gone. It lay in some forgotten alley, a tattered and dirty remnant of Thomas's past.

Thomas himself had forgotten all about it. In the world he now occupied, there was little time for quiet reflection. A street cat's aim is survival.

The weather had grown bleak and cold. He overheard someone say the streets were crowded because people were Christmas shopping. Every store window displayed a tree festooned with garlands and bright, shining balls. On street corners, strange looking men with white beards and ill-fitting red suits clanged large bells. Thomas wondered at it all, but his many questions went unanswered, for there was no one Thomas could ask.

He was constantly on the move, stopping only at night to sleep, and then always with one eye open and ears alert for signs of danger. Danger was one thing not in short supply for a kitten on the loose in the city.

"It's a jungle out there," Thomas had often heard Charlie Bradford remark to the family on his return home from his job in the city. Now Thomas knew what he meant.

He had experienced not one act of kindness during his travels. He had been stoned, kicked and doused with a

29

bucket of water by the two-legged animals he had encountered. As for the four-legged ones, he had barely escaped from some of them with his life.

He had been chased by snarling dogs, marauding tomcats, and once he had been cornered by a rat bigger than himself. Thomas calculated he had used up at least four of his allotted nine lives in the past month. His snow white fur was spotted with dirt, and the pink pads on his feet were dark with grime. Thomas knew Queenie would be ashamed to see her little prince reduced to a homeless vagabond.

The thought strengthened his resolve. He would find his way home no matter what it took, but his immediate concern was getting out of the city.

Thomas ducked under a parked car to think about the situation. The city must be a huge place, he decided. He had been traveling for four weeks, and he hadn't gotten through it yet. Automobiles though could travel many miles in a very short time. Hadn't Charlie Bradford traveled back and forth to the city every day in his automobile?

Thomas scurried out from under the car. He quickly looked around. People were hurrying, their heads were bent against the December wind, and none noticed him. He jumped up on the car's hood and squeezed through the partially open window. Settling down on the floor in the back of the car, he awaited the arrival of the owner.

An hour later the car door was opened, and a man got inside. He started the car, and they were off. Thomas discreetly sniffed the air. Something in the man's smell signaled a warning. This man was an enemy, one of that band of people Queenie had warned him about.

"There are certain people who have fixations about cats. They hate us with a consuming passion. A peculiar scent

30

surrounds these people, and you will know them immediately by it. Never let down your guard with them. They are extremely dangerous."

Queenie's warning rang in Thomas's ears. The fur prickled on his back, and his thin little body was overcome with a sudden chill.

They traveled for miles and miles and hours and hours, it seemed to Thomas. He was bone tired, but he dared not sleep. At last the car stopped. Thomas heard voices...

"Where you been at, Roy Johnson? I been settin here waitin for you."

"Hadda go to town," the man in the front seat answered.

The other man walked up to the car and stood leaning on the door talking to the one inside. Thomas could see him clearly from his hiding place on the floor. He was a rough looking man with an unkempt beard and bushy black eyebrows. He had a wad of tobacco in his mouth and punctuated each sentence with a loud spit.

"I wanna borrow your daug." Spit.

"Gonna do some rabbit huntin?"

"Yeah." Spit.

"Your welcome to 'im, but that ole hound ain't much good no more."

"Shoot, Roy. Might help if you'd feed him." Spit.

"He gets fed nuff. Just ornry. He's locked up in the barn. Go git im."

As the visitor walked away from the car, Thomas inched his way noiselessly up on the back seat so he could see outside.

31

They were parked in front of a run-down farmhouse. The man who Thomas now knew to be Roy Johnson remained in the front seat staring ahead as his friend walked back from the barn preceded by a large dog on a chain leash. Thomas quickly retreated to the floor.

"Shoot, Ray. This daug looks starved." Spit.

"Shut up and throw the hound in the back seat. I'll show yah how to hunt rabbits."

Thomas panicked. He could hide from humans, but there was no way he could hide from a dog. Already the animal was picking up his scent. Thomas could hear him whining in a high-pitched voice.

"What's the matter with that dumb daug?"

Thomas sprang from the floor to the seat and out the open window.

"What the..."

"Set that dog loose. That was a cat. Git that cat, you no-good hound."

Thomas sprinted across the field. His mind was racing as fast as his feet. The dog could outrun him and smell him out. He figured he had one chance—a tree. Thomas didn't reckon with the man's sadistic mind.

The dog was gaining on him. Thomas could hear the shouts of the men behind. "Git 'im. Come on, git that sucker."

Ahead, Thomas saw what he was looking for, a tall tree. He pushed forward with his last bit of strength as the dog nipped at his tail. Thomas made it up the tree to the very top.

When he looked down, the dog and both men were standing at the foot of the tree. Roy was hitting the yelping dog's head. "You dumb mutt."

The other man was laughing. "That's some huntin' daug you got there, Roy. Can't even outrun a half-growed cat. Wouldn't know what to do iffen he caught it anyhow, I speck."

"Oh yeah. You wanna see somethin? Stay here. I'll be right back."

Thomas watched as Roy Johnson walked back to the barn and went inside. He emerged a second later with a strange looking, long object over his arm.

"Whatcha gonna do? Shoot 'im down?"

"Jest gonna wing 'im and let the mutt finish 'im off. Ya ever see a dog tear a cat to pieces? Well, jest wait. You gonna see some fun."

Thomas had never seen a gun, and he didn't know what the word "shoot" meant.

A loud blast erupted from the object as the man pointed it, and Thomas felt a terrible, stinging pain in his foot. He held onto the branch, though. Now that he understood that pain, nothing would force him to drop from the tree. Painfully, he pulled himself along the branch, trying to get out of range. His ears rang with the barks of the dog and the shouts of the man. "You missed 'im."

"I only grazed him, but I'll get the sucker this time."

Thomas heard an approaching car and then the bearded man saying, "Hey, you in some kinda trouble, Roy?"

"Why?"

"A cop jest drove into your yard."

33

Roy Johnson put down the rifle and turned his attention away from Thomas. "Tell 'im I ain't home."

"But, your car's out there."

Thomas watched the policeman get out of his car. He called out in a loud voice, "Roy Johnson."

"Better see what he wants," the bearded man said.

Johnson answered, "Yeah, put the chain back on that fool dog. That's all I need—have him bite the cop."

When the men walked back to the front of the house, Thomas lost no time getting down and out of the tree. He crawled under a bush and looked at his foot. It was bleeding, and he licked it. *I must move on*, he thought. *I dare not rest until I put a safe distance between my enemies and me.*

Hopping on three legs, Thomas made his way painfully into the woods.

6

Nine Lives To Live

The wound on Thomas's paw had closed, but his leg throbbed constantly. The paw was twice its normal size, and Thomas felt as if his toes were on fire.

He lay on a pile of dried leaves and watched birds within his reach pecking for worms. It was impossible now for Thomas to hunt. But he did not give up. He had nine lives to live and was determined to live his full measure of time.

Forcing himself to move on, and stopping to rest so frequently that he covered little ground, it took Thomas two days to arrive at the other side of the woods.

He saw the house through eyes blurred by fever. An old two-story structure, which had been rebuilt and modernized haphazardly, was set back from the road. He blinked his eyes, half expecting the house to disappear, but it hadn't been a mirage. *Houses hold people,* he thought, *and where there are people, there is be food.* Lady Luck hadn't turned her back completely on Thomas Bradford.

Thomas made his way to the back of the house, where he expected to find the usual tall cans filled with discarded food. But there wasn't a trash can in sight. Thomas was puzzled. *The Bradfords had trash cans. The Martins had trash cans, and the alleys of the city contained nothing but trash cans. Don't people living in the country eat?*

Thomas darted under a bush as the back door suddenly opened and a woman stepped outside. She was older than Dottie Bradford, but not old old. Thomas decided this because her hair was yellow, not white. He had always thought that strange about humans—they had to be old to turn white-haired. He had been born white-haired.

The woman held a bowl from which she scattered something over the lawn. Then she went inside quickly, because it was very cold and she wore no coat.

As soon as the door closed, Thomas limped out from his hiding place and sniffed the ground. Bread!

Thomas gobbled up all the scattered pieces. When he had eaten the last piece, his radar ears picked up the sound of movement from inside the house. Looking up, he saw a cat staring at him through the window. She was black and white, and Thomas knew instinctively that she was a female and very old. Her eyes were still bright and alert, and she appeared to be studying Thomas, measuring him against some standard of which she alone was the judge. He resented the old cat's attention. She was warm and secure, on the inside looking out, and he was homeless, a crippled begger scrounging for a meal. He looked her straight in the eye with all the defiance of youth. Then he turned his back on her and walked proudly on his four legs out of her sight.

Later that same evening Thomas discovered why there were no trash cans behind this country home. A man came from the house carrying a bag filled with trash and deposited it in a contraption which Thomas later learned was called an "incinerator." Thomas watched as the man emptied the bag. When his nose picked up the scent of food, his stomach growled in protest.

"Well, what do you know? Where'd you come from, kitty?"

Thomas jumped back to the safety of the bush. Desperation had made him careless, and he scolded himself for being out in the open. He shrank back as the man approached him.

"Here, kitty, here kitty."

Fear overwhelmed Thomas. Faces of all the humans he had encountered since leaving home loomed before him, culminating in the cruel, leering face of Roy Johnson. Thomas's ears went back on his head, and he emitted a long, low growl.

A huge hand poked through the bush and groped around. Terrified, Thomas flattened himself against the thick branches. The big hand grabbed Thomas by the scuff of the neck and pulled him.

Thomas went wild. He unsheathed his claws and dug. The hand was pulled back quickly. "Ow—you devil, you."

"What's wrong?" a female voice called from the house.

"There's a kitten out here, but it's wild. Just leave it be, Marcy. These feral cats can be dangerous. It got me good on the hand."

The man went back to the house, and Thomas crouched low, his eyes glued to the man's retreating figure. Not until the door closed and the man had disappeared into the house did Thomas relax his vigilance.

The man had called him a "feral" cat. Thomas didn't know what that meant, but the man said they were dangerous.

And I am dangerous, Thomas told himself. *I'll bite and claw any human who tries to catch me. Humans are mean, and I'll never trust another one, only the Bradfords. They*

*have to be the only decent humans in the whole world, and
I have to find them, even if it takes all of my lives to do it.*

♋   ♋   ♋

A blanket of snow partially covered the little body of
Thomas Bradford. He was neither cold, nor hot, nor even
in pain from his swollen leg. Hunger and fear, his ever-
present companions had deserted him, and the angel of death
beckoned to him and promised him the serenity of unending
sleep. Thomas felt himself slipping into the last stage of
acceptance when the door to the house burst open, and voices
shattered the icy stillness.

"Here kitty—here kitty."

"He won't come, Marcy. I told you he's a feral cat.
You can't tame them."

"Nonsense, Drew. What are feral cats anyway, but house
cats that have been mistreated and abandoned? Where was
he when you saw him?"

"Under that bush, but you don't expect to find him there
now, do you? Marcy, that cat's long gone."

The woman peered under the bush, but Thomas's
whiteness created a perfect camouflage against the snow.

"Here kitty, here kitty," she called louder.

"Come on, Marcy. He's not here now."

"Oh, Drew. He'll die if we don't find him. They're
predicting another two feet of snow tonight."

The woman's words, "he'll die," echoed in Thomas's
sub-conscious mind and every fiber of his being shouted,
"No!"

He couldn't give up, not him, not Thomas Bradford, son of a king. Thomas opened his mouth and cried out as loudly as he could. Then, he lost consciousness.

7

Sheba's Wacky Family

Very slowly, Thomas emerged from his deep sleep. Gradually his senses returned. He sniffed the air and knew that he was inside a house, resting on a soft pillow in a large basket like the one he was born in. He moved his tongue and felt the familiar taste of his own whiskers. His leg still throbbed, but it was the gentle throb of healing muscles. His eyes remained closed, but he heard the sound of voices:

"Sir Percival, unhand me! Blackguard, cad. I shall never consent. Never, never. Don't close that door. Oh, dear God in heaven, he's leaving me here in this dark place, in this dungeon with the rats! Oh, no, please, please."

Thomas's weary brain was galvanized into action. Where was he? If Sir Whats-his-name was leaving her in the dungeon with the rats, Thomas must be there, too, and he wasn't up to fighting rats.

His eyes opened in terror, but he saw no rats. He saw no dungeon or even a dark place. He surveyed his surroundings and saw only an ordinary room.

There was a desk, and seated at the desk was the woman. The man had called her "Marcy." It was she who had been talking, but there was no Sir Percival. There was only the old cat, sitting right on the desk, staring calmly at the hysterical woman. Next to the cat was a strange looking box, and the woman was talking directly into it.

40

"Oh, I shall die. I shall die down here."

"Marcia."

Thomas jerked his head toward the sound of a second voice. Another woman was standing in the doorway. She was old, like the cat, but her hair was blue instead of white.

The woman at the desk turned and said, "Mother, I'm working."

"Well, turn that thing off. I just stopped in for a minute. I'm going to town."

"In this weather?"

"One can't stay cooped up all winter just because of a a little snow."

"It's the blizzard of 1998, Mother."

"They call everything a blizzard today."

The woman came into the room then and sat down. Thomas raised his head slightly for a closer look at the newcomer.

The woman wore a sapphire blue coat with a large blue fox collar which she removed and slung over a chair. She was still covered in blue, though, for under the coat was a blue dress.

"What are you working on?" she asked.

"*Sir Percival's Revenge.*"

"Oh, did you finish, *Sir Percival's Dilemma*?"

"Of course. I sent it to three publishers."

The Blue Lady picked up a stack of papers from the desk and scanned the pages. "Your heroine's dull."

"What do you mean, Mother? How could you know? You just glanced at the first page."

"Exactly. Listen—Amanda was a small brown-eyed girl. Her thick, chestnut-colored hair was parted in the middle and pulled back from her face into a braided knot."

"So?"

"So—brown eyes, brown hair, a braided knot. She's a mouse, I'd say."

"She is not a mouse, Mother. The year is 1836. What would you have me do? Put her in spit curls and a mini-skirt?"

"Certainly not. Spit curls belong to flappers. I should know. I was one myself. Now, that's the age you should write about, Marcia—the twenties. Oh, what a time it was. You wouldn't even have to research the period. I could tell you anything you'd want to know. The styles, the dances..."

To Thomas's amazement, the Blue Lady suddenly kicked off her shoes and demonstrated a lively dance step.

"I can still do a mean Charleston," she said and collapsed breathless in a chair.

"Terrific, but unfortunately Gothic novels aren't set in the twenties, Mother."

"Too bad, but I still say change that heroine. You know, Marcia, you have to have..."

"I know, Mother—a gimmick. You've told me that before."

"It's true. Take Scarlett O'Hara. Everybody remembers that she had green eyes and raven-black hair. Mousey? No way. Then there was Amber, a heroine with amber eyes. Did you ever see a woman with amber eyes, Marcia? Of course not, but people remember Amber. Get rid of that brown hair, I say. I like the title though. *Sir Percival's Revenge*—that ought to make readers curious."

"I'm glad you approve of something."

"Oh, don't be so touchy, Marcia. What was his revenge, anyway?"

"When you read the book, you'll find out."

"Do you know what it is yet?"

"Of course."

"You won't tell me?"

"No, I won't tell you."

They laughed then, and the Blue Lady changed the subject abruptly. "Where's your new cat?"

Thomas closed his eyes and hoped he looked unconscious. *New cat, like fun,* he thought. He wasn't going to be her new cat. He'd be on his way again as soon as he was strong enough to travel. True, they had saved his life, but that didn't entitle them to own him. They were probably good people, he conceded, but crazy as loons. And that old cat—she was something else, looking at Thomas like she was so superior. *Don't worry, old queen. I don't want your home or your wacky family.*

"Ah, poor thing. He's so thin."

They stood looking down on him, and Thomas kept his eyes tightly shut.

"I know, but Winston says he'll be OK. He gave him a shot for the infection, and he'll probably sleep all day."

"I hope Winston knows what he's doing. He's been retired five years."

"Mother, the man was a well-known veterinarian. We're lucky to have him for a neighbor. Incidentally, he was disappointed that he didn't see you last night."

"Pooh, that old fool."

43

A faint rustle told Thomas they had taken their leave, and he opened his eyes and then quickly shut them, but he was too late. The Blue Lady had seen him.

"He's come to, Marcia. He just opened his eyes and would you believe it, he's odd-eyed." The Blue Lady was very excited. "Now, that's your gimmick," she said.

"An odd-eyed cat?"

"Certainly not. An odd-eyed heroine. Make the little brown mouse have odd-eyes. It's positively ingenious."

"It's positively insane, Mother."

"That's the trouble with you, Marcia. You have no imagination, no flair."

"This is a Gothic romance, Mother, not science fiction. An odd-eyed heroine! Oh, you're impossible."

Thomas slowly opened his eyes, but they were no longer looking at him. They were too involved in their argument. The Blue Lady put on her coat.

"I'm leaving, but give my idea some thought. It's not my advice, you know."

"I remember. A Hollywood agent told you that in 1933. He said, 'Get a gimmick, girl.'"

"That's right, he did, and the very next day I appeared in his office all dressed in blue from the tips of my new blue shoes to the top of my blue-dyed hair, and he said, 'Terrific, kid. From now on, your name's Beula Blue, and I'm gonna make you a star.' And, he almost did, only I eloped with your father instead. The good advice still stands though, Marcia."

"I'll give it serious thought, Mother."

When the Blue Lady had gone, Marcia spoke to the old cat. "What do you think, Sheba? Am I wasting my time? Thirty-five novels on Sir Percival's adventures and not one, not even one, published!

CHAPTER

8

Christmas In The Country

Thomas recovered quickly. Marcia Collins gave the credit to old Doc Winston's emergency treatment the night Thomas was found in the snow, but Thomas knew that without Marcy's care, he would not have made it.

She called him "Snow," which Thomas thought was rather corny, but then it was certainly better than "Shirley." *I wouldn't be staying with them long, anyway,* he told himself. Physically, he was already strong enough to leave, but the weather was against him. It was bitter cold, and Thomas heard Drew say it was a hard winter.

They were, all of them, good to him, particularly Marcy. He tolerated her fussing over him. He let her stroke him and hold him, even when she called him her "Snow Baby," but he held himself aloof from all of them. Having been hurt so badly by humans, Thomas erected a barrier against them.

He had been with the Collins family several weeks before he learned that there were two additional members who did not live in the house with Marcy, Drew and Beula. They were Marcy and Drew's children, Zorita and Dashiell.

Zorita was the older of the two. She was a teacher, and she lived and worked in another town. Dash Collins was twenty, and he attended a very expensive college called Harvard. Thomas knew it was expensive because the family frequently discussed this aspect of the school. Thomas

46

gathered from family conversations that money, or the immediate lack of it, was a source of much concern, especially for the man, Drew Collins.

Both of these absent family members were expected to arrive home at any moment for something called "the holidays." Thomas was curious about the holidays, but he refused to show his ignorance before the old cat, Sheba. They had an armed truce. Sheba had territorial rights, and she let Thomas know it from the very beginning.

Thomas watched the frantic preparations that the humans made for the coming event. The man cut down a big tree and brought it right into the house. Thomas was certain the two women would give him a good tongue lashing for doing so. He knew Dottie Bradford would never have allowed such a thing inside her house, but to Thomas's amazement, the Blue Lady and Marcy seemed proud of it and that night they hung colored balls and silver rope on it.

They spent a lot of time in the kitchen baking cookies. One day they made a fruit cake and poured on it a bottle of the same foul smelling stuff the wino in the alley had used. Thomas left the room.

The daughter, Zorita, was first to arrive home. She looked like Marcy, only she was younger. Thomas had heard them say she was twenty-five, which for a human was considered young.

Zorita made a big fuss over old Sheba, and Thomas gathered that old Sheba had been given to Zorita as a kitten. Then they told Zorrie about the new cat, and Thomas took advantage of Marcy's long-winded account to look for a good hiding place. Of course, Zorrie wanted to see him, and Thomas was amused watching the three of them crawling around the floor searching under tables and chairs while he observed them from the top of the buffet.

Eventually, of course, Thomas relented and allowed himself to be found. He submitted to the inevitable petting and fussing. Humans, particularly female ones, acted rather ridiculous over him at times, but it had little effect on Thomas, because he had closed his heart to all except the Bradfords.

Dash Collins arrived home several days later. He was an extremely handsome young man with deep blue eyes and very fair, silver blond hair. It was plain to see the whole family doted on him. Something about Dash vaguely disturbed Thomas, and yet, at the same time, Thomas felt a strange kinship with the young man.

The night before the grand holiday, the family brought red stockings downstairs and hung them over the fireplace. Thomas thought this rather peculiar, particularly when he observed Marcy putting all kinds of nonsensical things inside them—including toothpaste and candy bars.

Sheba took her accustomed place on the sofa and Thomas curled up for the night under the dining room table to await the big day.

He was not disappointed. To his surprise, one of the stockings was for him. Identical to Sheba's, it contained a catnip mouse, a rubber ball and a can of sardines.

Thomas watched as the humans exchanged gifts, and it was obvious, even to him, that Dash received the best presents. Thomas supposed that was because he wouldn't be going back to Harvard next term. Of course, Dash didn't know that yet, but Thomas had overheard Marcy and Drew discussing the problem one night in their bedroom:

"I can't swing it anymore. Dash will just have to understand," said Drew.

"Oh, Drew. He'll be so disappointed."

"I'm sorry, but it won't be the end of the world. He can transfer to State."

"Don't tell him yet. Maybe things will change."

"Marcy, try to understand. Nothing's going to change. The company's been sold, and they have their own man. I'm out. They're being generous. I can stay until March and then its, 'thanks, old man, for 25 good years. Good luck finding something else.' And, what do you suppose I can find, Marcy. I'm fifty, and I'm all washed up."

"Don't say that, Drew. Something will turn up, and if I sell, *Sir Percival's Dilemma*, we'll be on easy street."

Thomas knew nothing about *Sir Percival's Dilemma*, but he had been listening to *Sir Percival's Revenge* every day, and he didn't exactly share Marcy's optimism.

A bright fire blazed in the hearth, while outside another snowfall dressed the fields and trees in shimmering white. The human's big day was drawing to a close.

Sheba napped close to the fire, and Thomas dozed several feet away. The family had eaten their festive meal, and Thomas had been given his first taste of turkey.

Doc Winston had joined them for dinner. A quiet man and naturally shy, he seldom socialized since his wife's death, but Marcy in her zany way had a rare gift for putting even the shyest at ease, and Winston Porterfield was having the time of his life.

The Blue Lady was telling him about her Hollywood days and Winston was spellbound. He was an old movie buff. Once or twice he got a word in edgewise and Thomas heard

49

him say, "When I was in college, I was quite a fan of the cinema. I particularly liked Carol Lombard."

"Oh, Grandmom has the movie star album," Dash said and he and Zorita joined the Blue Lady and Doc Winston in pouring over the old pictures. Most of them were of the Blue Lady.

"Twenty-three skidoo. Will you look at Grandmom in this outfit," Zorrie said.

"That was the night I won the Charleston contest," the Blue Lady explained, and Thomas's natural curiosity got the better of him.

He sauntered over and sat next to Zorrie so he could see the pictures, too.

"Hey, look, the new cat wants to look at your picture," Dash said.

Doc Winston patted Thomas on the head. "They can't distinguish pictures or colors," he told them.

Thomas looked at the picture. He saw a young girl with short, tousled curls. A silver band encircled her forehead, and her eyes danced with merriment. Her dress was very short with row upon row of black fringe on the skirt. She was posed as if caught in the middle of a dance step. Thomas knew in terms of human pulchtritude, she would have been considered quite a dish.

"You were something else, Grandmom," Dash said.

Old Doc Winston stammered. "Your grandmother was a great beauty. Still is, I might add."

Then he coughed, and Thomas thought to himself, *you might think I can't tell colors, but I sure can see the color of your face, and it is red.*

50

Later, after Doc Winston had gone home, and the older members of the family had gone to bed, Zorrie and Dash brought up their old sleds from the basement and went out in the snow.

They came back about an hour later, bringing with them the freshness of the icy air outside. Then they sat on the floor in front of the fire to talk.

"How're all the little people in third grade?" Dash asked his sister.

"Fine. I like teaching and some of these children come from such disadvantaged backgrounds. It's very rewarding when you can see that little spark that let's you know you've gotten through to them."

"I guess so. You've got a good heart, Zorrie, but you should think more about yourself."

"What do you mean? I'm doing what I like. What's better than that?"

"Making lots of money."

"I'll leave you to be the tycoon in the family."

"This family sure could use one."

"Why do you say that?"

"Dad might be out of a job soon. Don't say anything, but Allied has been bought out by Republic International. Chuck Lawrence, at school, is a friend of mine, and his father just happens to be a VP with Republic. Chuck said that Republic always brings in their own men when they take over a company, so..."

"Poor Dad. I wish they hadn't spent so much on Christmas."

"Just so things hold out till I'm finished at Harvard. The contacts I'm making there will stand me for life."

"Don't worry so much about success, Dash. Happiness is more important."

"You think so? Well, I don't. I don't want to be like the rest of this family."

"What's wrong with the family?"

"Aw, you know, Zorrie. Mom and her stories—none of them will ever get published. She must have a room full of manuscripts by now and still she keeps on writing and hoping. Grandmom, who never made it in Hollywood. Dad, stuck in the same job for twenty-five years."

"Don't knock them, Dash. That one book—I can't remember the title, but it was almost published by Tower."

"And Grandmom was ALMOST a movie star fifty years ago. Dad ALMOST got a big promotion ten years ago. I don't want ALMOST, Zorrie. That's not good enough for me."

Thomas drifted off to sleep with their voices droning on in the background. Again, he felt a weird kinship with Dash Collins. It left him feeling disturbed, but the reason for it eluded him.

9

Outsmarting The Swindler

It was a long, hard winter. Snow covered the ground from December through February. Old Sheba caught a cold, and Marcy was so worried about her, she brought Doc Winston out in the middle of a snowstorm.

"She's fifteen, Marcy. That's mighty old for a cat," he said, and then looking at Marcy's stricken face added, "but, some cats live into their twenties. Don't worry, we'll pull the old girl through." Then he reached into his black bag and brought out a big needle. Thomas retreated to the basement at the sight of it. He remembered getting a needle.

Marcy brought up the basket that had been Thomas's bed when he was sick and lined it with a soft, wool blanket, but old Sheba would have no part of it. She preferred sleeping curled up on the couch or under one of the beds upstairs. All work on *Sir Percival's Revenge* came to a dead stop.

Thomas overheard Marcy tell Drew, "I know it sounds silly, but I can't write without Sheba. For some reason, I need her sitting on that desk listening, to get my creative juices flowing."

Sir Percival's Dilemma was rejected by the publisher. They sent it back with a printed card attached. "After careful consideration, we find this manuscript is not right for our list. Thank you for your submission."

Marcy read the card. Then she paced the floor very quickly, up and down, back and forth three times with her head down and her hands clasped behind her back. Then she picked up the manuscript and hurled it across the room. She said, "Idiots—fools. What do they know?"

Thomas was frightened. He had never seen Marcy act this way before. He looked at Sheba, but the old cat was calmly washing her paws. Thomas crawled under a small table and watched as Marcy proceeded to pull all the books out of the bookcase and slam them on the floor. "You got published," she said, each time she pulled one out.

When the bookcase was empty and the floor was littered with books, Marcy sat on the floor in the middle of the whole mess and cried.

At this point, old Sheba stood up, stretched herself and calmly sauntered over to the desk. She sprang to the top of it with surprising alacrity and sat in her usual spot.

Marcy and Sheba stared at each other for several seconds, and then Marcy stood up, brushed herself off and started picking the books up and replacing them in the bookcase.

She walked over to the desk, sat down and said, "Chapter 12—Sir Percival deposited his diamond-studded cane in the stand, slowly peeled off his gloves and removed his heavy black cape. He tossed it on the floor with a flourish, and an evil smile crossed his face. 'Now, my proud Amanda,' he said."

Later that day Thomas saw Marcy pick up the discarded manuscript from the floor, dust it off and place it in a fresh brown envelope. She paused, tapping her pen on the desk for a moment, then smiled and said, "Baker and Fields. I'll send it to them. I've never tried a hard-cover publisher before."

54

She was humming happily as she passed Thomas on her way to the post office. Thomas was glad that Marcy was herself again. *There is one thing to be said for living in this house,* he thought. *It certainly is never dull.*

When Marcy came back, she was very excited. She called upstairs to the Blue Lady, "Mother, come here quick. Look what was in the mail."

Thomas was curious, so he followed them into the Family Room and listened. The Blue Lady read the letter out loud.

"Dear Writer: Having trouble getting published? We'd like to help. Our representative will be in your vicinity the week of February 15th. Take advantage of this opportunity to discuss your manuscript with us. We have helped countless new writers to get published. Fame and fortune can be yours if your manuscript meets our standards. Call us toll free for an appointment."

"What do you think?" Marcy asked.

"I think you should call right now and make the appointment. Opportunity knocks but once and how well I know it. I was almost a star, but then your father—but, he was worth it. None of my other husbands could match him...."

Marcy made the call and the appointment was set up for the following week. When she put down the phone, she said, "Don't say anything to Drew, Mother. He's been so down in the dumps. I don't want to give him any false hopes, but if this works out, all our troubles will be over. Oh, I'm so excited."

The Blue Lady was excited, too, and she said, "I hope they make it into a movie. I can just see us at the premiere, flashbulbs flashing, the crowds, the TV reporters. Oh, I wonder if anybody will remember me?"

♋   ♋   ♋

The air crackled with excitement on the appointed day. Marcy changed her clothes three times before deciding, contrary to her mother's opinion, to wear a simple skirt and blouse.

The Blue Lady was going out. She felt Marcy should see the representative alone, but her curiosity wouldn't let her leave until after the man arrived. They had kept the meeting a secret from Drew, and as soon as he left for work, they had raced to the attic to bring down all 35 copies of Marcy's manuscripts.

"He's here," the Blue Lady called from her post at the window.

Thomas jumped up on the windowsill to see a man with a briefcase emerge from a long, black car.

"I'll open the door," the Blue Lady said.

Marcy seated herself at her desk to await the caller. The 35 manuscripts were piled, some on the desk, some on the floor and some on chairs all around the room.

Sheba, sensing the importance of the occasion, jumped up on the desk and Thomas crawled into an open file drawer where he could see—but not be seen by—the caller.

The man was small in stature with a thin, black moustache which looked like it had been drawn on his lip with a pencil. The Blue Lady ushered him into Marcy's office.

"Here is the author," she said importantly. "Marcia, Mr. Cottonwood of Cottonwood Press."

56

The Blue Lady left on her trumped up errand and Marcy and Mr. Cottonwood sat facing each other across Marcy's cluttered desk.

"Now, Mrs. Collins, let's discuss your manuscript."

"Of course. Which manuscript are you interested in?"

"Ah, a prolific writer. I like that. How many manuscripts have you completed?"

"Thirty-five and I'm working on another one."

Mr. Cottonwood appeared at a loss for words, but Marcy continued gaily on. "I brought them all down, and I tried to keep them in sequence." Picking up a thick manuscript from her desk, she said, This is *Sir Percival's Misfortune.*" She reached for another one. "*Sir Percival's Secret.* Oh, I know the first one is here somewhere. Mr. Cottonwood, would you mind?—Right there on the floor beside you, what is the title of that manuscript?"

Mr. Cottonwood leaned over and peered down. "*Sir Percival Pettigrew I,*" he read.

"That's it. That's the beginning."

"You mean—you mean all these manuscripts are one continuous story?"

"No, certainly not. Each one is complete in itself."

Mr. Cottonwood appeared relieved. "Well now, Mrs. Collins, since each is complete in itself, why don't you just select the one you prefer."

"Well, I guess we should start at the beginning, shouldn't we? Oh, I don't know. I wrote that—how many years ago? Let's see, Sheba is fifteen and she was about two when I started writing—that would be thirteen years ago. Thirteen is bad luck, so maybe not that one."

57

A look of impatience crossed Mr. Cottonwood's face, but Marcy was not looking at him. She was intent on the manuscripts. *"Sir Percival's Secret.* My daughter really liked that one. She's a teacher and she was in college when I..."

"Mrs. Collins, perhaps the last one would be best. All writers improve as they go on. Let's settle on *Sir Percival's*—er—um. what did you call it?"

"Sir Percival's Dilemma."

"Of course, excellent choice for a title. It has a ring to it. Yes, indeed it does. Now then, shall we go with this last one Mrs. Collins?"

"Whatever you think."

"Fine. The last shall be first then—ha ha."

Old Sheba opened her mouth and yawned at this point, displaying a still formidable array of teeth, and Mr. Cottonwood apparently noticed her presence for the first time. "Oh, you have a cat. I didn't see it at first. Sits right there on the desk, eh?"

"This is Sheba," Marcy said. "She really helps me with my writing."

Mr. Cottonwood gave Marcy an incredulous look, but he didn't pursue the subject.

"Our bindings are beautiful, Mrs. Collins and I've brought some samples for your selection."

"But, don't you have to read the manuscript first?"

"Read the manuscript?"

"To see if I qualify. If it meets your standards. The letter said..."

"Of course, of course, Mrs. Collins. I intend taking it along with me, but this is just to save time. If we can get these preliminaries out of the way today, well then, we can move right along to publish your book. If you qualify, of course."

Thomas was watching old Sheba. She was sniffing the air, and the pupils of her eyes were dilating to large black circles. Thomas sniffed the air, too and caught the scent. It was coming from Mr. Cottonwood, and it was growing stronger as he talked. Marcy was completely unaware of it, for it was one of the those scents that are undetectable to humans, but Thomas and Sheba recognized it immediately. Mr. Cottonwood was not to be trusted!

Sheba changed her position, and Mr. Cottonwood glanced quickly toward her. Another scent wafted across the air and told Thomas something else about Mr. Cottonwood. He was afraid of cats.

Things started happening very fast at that point. Mr. Cottonwood produced a long document from his briefcase. "This is our contract. It gives us the authority to publish the manuscript. Now, if we can get this signed while I'm here, we'll be that much further ahead, Mrs. Collins."

"But, suppose after you read the manuscript..."

"Suppose I find it not good enough, you mean? Well then naturally, Mrs. Collins, we won't sign our part of the agreement."

"Oh, I see. You want me to sign and then after you review the manuscript..."

"Exactly, Mrs. Collins. Here, take my pen. Just sign on the dotted line."

Old Sheba suddenly jumped down from the desk and onto the arm of the chair where Mr. Cottonwood sat. All of the color drained out of his face, and his body stiffened.

Marcy laughed. "Sheba probably wants to see it, too. She's been in on the Sir Percival novels from the beginning."

Mr. Cottonwood wasn't laughing. All of his savoir faire evaporated, and he groped for words. "Mrs. Collins, suppose I just leave the contract with you for now. You can mail it back. I do have another appointment."

"No, I can sign it now."

Thomas jumped out of the file cabinet and sprang to the other arm of Mr. Cottonwood's chair, and Mr. Cottonwood looked faint. "You have two cats? How nice," he said weakly.

"That's Snow," Marcy said proudly. "He's a half-grown kitten. He was a stray—a feral cat, really, but we love him dearly."

"What's a feral cat?" Mr. Cottonwood asked.

"A wild cat," Marcy said simply.

Mr. Cottonwood appeared to shrink a little. "Wild," he repeated in a small voice.

"Look at his eyes," Marcy told him. "They're different. One is blue and one is yellow."

Mr. Cottonwood looked at Thomas. Thomas crossed his eyes, a trick he had learned from Mark Bradford. Then he curled his lip to show his long, needle sharp teeth.

Sheba, for her part, emitted a long, low growl, and Mr. Cottonwood jumped. "I must be going. I'll be in touch, Mrs. Collins."

Hastily gathering his samples, he stuffed them into his briefcase and snapping the case shut, he reached for his coat, all the while keeping a wary eye on the two cats.

"Oh, the manuscript—you forgot the manuscript," Marcy cried, but Mr. Cottonwood was already out in the hall and heading for the front door. Marcy hurried after him, and he grabbed the manuscript from her hand and bolted to his car.

Alone in the office, Thomas and Sheba looked at each other. Sheba got down on the floor and rolled with silent feline laughter. Thomas had never known Sheba to forget her dignity, but recalling the pasty face of Mr. Cottonwood, Thomas laughed too, and being young, he found it harder to control himself, once he had started.

He rolled and rolled and laughed and laughed until Marcy's scolding voice brought him sharply back to reality. Like most humans, she thought he was having a cat fit, "Stop that, Snowbaby, you'll make yourself sick."

Thomas stood up abruptly and when he noticed old Sheba, dignity intact, staring at him with lanquid, yellow eyes, he became embarrassed and pretended to be washing his paws.

♋   ♋   ♋

Marcy never heard from Mr. Cottonwood. She spent the following week feeling despondant over it, certain that it was because *Sir Percival's Dilemma* had failed to qualify and was unworthy of publication.

The Blue Lady tried to encourage her. "You certainly can't expect to hear after only a few weeks. The man had other appointments scheduled. He even told you so."

61

Mr. Cottonwood had, in fact, scheduled quite a few appointments in the area. As it turned out, Marcy was luckier than the others, according to the police who stopped by in the course of their investigation.

It seemed that Mr. Cottonwood was a crook, which came as no surprise to either Sheba or Thomas, but the news left both the Blue Lady and Marcy flabbergasted.

Mr. Cottonwood had worked his scheme in several states, managing to swindle a long list of budding novelists out of substantial sums. The police were at a loss to understand why he had not even broached the subject of money with Marcy, but concluded that perhaps he meant to gain her confidence.

Marcy only knew that Mr. Cottonwood suddenly appeared to remember another appointment and that she even had to remind him to take her manuscript with him.

"It was almost a dream come true," she commented sadly after the police had gone. Her words reminded Thomas of the conversation he had overheard between Zorrie and Dash at Christmas when Dash had scorned the family for their "almost" accomplishments.

"Nothing ventured, nothing gained," the Blue Lady said safely. "No harm's been done. You haven't gained, but then you haven't lost anything either."

"No," Marcy agreed, managing to smile. "Everything is just the same."

And it was. Marcy went right back to work on *Sir Percival's Revenge* with Sheba at the helm. The brief camaraderie between Sheba and Thomas—which had blossomed during the Mr. Cottonwood crisis—ended, and they resumed their former relationship.

Everything was the same, but somehow different now, Thomas thought. He kept remembering Dash's comments, and he compared the Collins family with the Bradfords. The Bradfords were definitely achievers, he concluded, and "almost" was not in their vocabulary. He'd be happy to be home with them again, but Marcy's wistful face kept intruding on his thoughts and when it did, a strange, uncomfortable feeling came too.

ᏉᏉ ᏉᏉ ᏉᏉ

Several days later another crisis struck. Drew Collins got the axe. Thomas didn't understand that part of it, but the fact that he no longer had a job was clear. Drew was very depressed, and he spent a lot of time out by the incinerator, talking to himself.

Marcy was overly cheerful and even ventured to say it was a blessing in disguise, and that now Drew would find something even better, but Drew just shook his head and continued to vent his frustrations outside the house with only Thomas, Sheba and the incinerator for an audience.

Marcy was worried about Dash, and she confided to the Blue Lady, "Dash will have to leave Harvard, and I just don't know how he'll take it, Mother."

The Blue Lady predicted that Dash would accept the bad news with good grace. "He can always say he went to Harvard and almost graduated from there," she suggested.

Thomas listened and knew right away that Dash would never, under any circumstances be an "almost." He would be home for Easter, and the secret would be told then. Thomas's secret would be discovered at the same time, for Thomas had decided he would leave right after the holidays.

10

Two For The Road

Angry voices drifted down to the living room where Thomas and Sheba were napping, Sheba on the hearth and Thomas, a few feet away. The family argument was upsetting Thomas's plans. He and Sheba usually were let outside for a run before bedtime, and when they would return, Marcy always had a bowl of milk waiting for them. Tonight Thomas had planned not to return.

He knew Marcy would worry and probably stay up calling and calling him until Drew would convince her to come to bed. Thomas didn't like to think about how disappointed Marcy would be when her "Snowbaby" would fail to turn up the next day.

But that's the way the cookie crumbles, he said to himself flippantly, using one of Mark Bradford's favorite expressions.

Now, though, it seemed he wasn't going to be given the opportunity to make his getaway as planned, because the argument upstairs had Marcy so unsettled she had forgotten all about letting the cats out.

Dash and his father were going at it hot and heavy about Harvard. Dash had not, as the Blue Lady predicted, taken the bad news with good grace. On the contrary, Dash had refused to transfer to the state university, calling it a second-rate school, and he had practically demanded that his father get a bank loan to put him through his final year at Harvard.

Poor Marcy had tried to keep the peace, and she brought up *Sir Percival's Dilemma* and promised that if the book got published, she'd see that Dash went back to Harvard.

Dash was too exasperated to consider his mother's feelings and answered her sarcastically. "If I have to wait for *Sir Percival* to get published, I'll be too old for Harvard, Mother."

This was too much for Drew. He lost his temper and shouted, "Grow up, Dash! If you want Harvard so much, get out and work and send yourself to Harvard!"

"Fine," Dash answered. "I'll leave right now. I'll make it on my own. I don't need your money."

A door slammed and several minutes later, Dash raced down the stairs, suitcase in hand. Marcy and Zorita followed at his heels. Marcy was crying, and Zorrie called, "Dash, don't do this. What is wrong with you? Can't you see what you're doing to Mom?"

Dash never stopped. He opened the front door, and Thomas ran out, too. Dash jumped into his car and soon was speeding away from the house. Thomas looked back, and saw Zorrie and Marcy framed in the doorway. Zorrie closed the door, and it was then that Thomas realized Sheba was beside him.

"You're leaving, too, aren't you?" she communicated to him in her soft, gutteral voice.

Thomas eyed her defiantly and thought, *What does she care? Besides, she never wants to share her place with me.*

"Stay," Sheba said simply. "I'll be leaving soon, and they'll need you."

Crazy old cat, Thomas thought. *Where does she think she's going anyway? She couldn't last a day on her own.* He stared contemptuously at her frail body and then turned his back on her and sprinted into the woods.

Old Sheba looked back to the house. All of the lights were out. She looked toward the sky. The April moon was lost in the clouds and the sudden patter of rain sent her scurrying for shelter. She dived under the porch and curled her thin body into a tight ball, but the rain sought her out and soaked her fur without mercy.

♋   ♋   ♋

This journey would be very different from the one that had brought Thomas, starving and wounded, to Marcy's door in the midst of a snowstorm.

Thomas was nine months old now, almost full grown. His added size and strength helped him cover open country, and the soft spring days offered no hardship weatherwise. But in the city, there would be new dangers to face—dangers that Thomas had not encountered as a kitten.

Thomas was enjoying the life of a vagabond. Food was plentiful, birds and small game abounded, and Thomas proved to be a good hunter. He distained his old habit of scrounging in garbage cans, but he knew when he reached the city, he would have to scrounge or steal his food again.

Thomas was tempted to forget his mission and become a real feral cat, living a wild and free existence without dependence on any human, but he was also obsessed with returning to his origins. He wanted to see Queenie again, and his father. Most of all, he wanted to establish his own identity. Thomas was a prince, and he was destined to fulfill a proud heritage. Either he would become, like his father, a king among cats, or he would deign to grace the home of a family as Queenie had done.

However, if he was to live with any humans, they would have to be extraordinary humans. The Martins, of course, had been out of the question—a blow-bag for a father, a whiner of a mother, and that impossible little girl who had called him "Shirley."

The Collins family had been good to him, but they were by no means extraordinary people. In fact, they were failures, all of them, except maybe for Dash, and he had yet to prove himself. And then there was old Sheba, the prima cat who acted like she was royalty. That was a big laugh. Thomas smiled to himself just thinking about it.

The Bradfords, of course, were extraordinary people. Dottie Bradford was a recognized authority on Siamese cats, and she was an officer in the Chesapeake Cat Association. Charlie Bradford was a successful lawyer, and Mark and Judy both were achievers. But it had been fun staying the winter with the madcap Collins family, he admitted, and then quickly thought of something else.

It was summer before Thomas reluctantly turned his attention to the matter at hand—the search for his lost family. He had put off entering the city with all its people, cars, and garbage cans, but he had to retrace his steps.

Thomas returned to the scene of his early hardships. The run-down neighborhood of cheap bars and greasy restaurants had not changed at all. But Thomas Bradford had changed. The frightened, half-starved little kitten was now, thanks to Mother Nature and Marcy's good food, a healthy, strong cat, well on his way to being as powerful as his father.

Thomas headed for the long alley behind the shops. His thoughts were on the juicy steak he expected to snatch for

67

his dinner. He located the restaurant and hopped up on the window sill as before. The same white-coated chef was busy at the cutting board. This time he was cutting chicken and then transferring the pieces to a deep fryer. Thomas wasn't hard to please; chicken would do just as well as steak.

He leaped from the window sill to the closest garbage can, knocking it over with ease. The irate chef burst through the door as Thomas had expected, cursing and screaming at his imaginary hoodlums. In a flash, Thomas was in and out, dragging half a chicken with him.

As before, the feat was accomplished in less than five minutes, and Thomas dragged his prize around the corner to the exact spot as before to feast upon it. Now, however, the scenerio sharply changed. Thomas heard a low growl. Looking up, he saw another cat poised on the fence.

It was a full-grown, coal black male. Probably a poor diet and bad living conditions had stunted its growth so that it was not much bigger than Thomas. The challenger seemed tough and street-wise, and he wanted Thomas's chicken.

Thomas contined to eat, tearing the raw chicken apart with his strong teeth. He did not look up at the other cat.

The old tom was surprised. This wasn't going to be easy, after all. He measured his opponent. The stranger was young, a house cat, judging from the rich coat and well-fed body, but house cats were soft, experience had taught him. The street cat jumped from the fence and landed on sure feet directly in front of Thomas.

Though Thomas was a novice, he recognized the act as a prelude to battle. In that instant, he remembered Macy's voice dictating into the machine: *Sir Percival slipped off his glove and struck the Black Knight across the face with it.*

68

Now there was no turning back. They would duel to the death.

Thomas looked into his adversary's face. Fierce yellow eyes stared back at him. A long scar ran across the street cat's nose, giving him a satanic look. Patches of fur were missing from his body and the smell of his breath reached Thomas's delicate nostrils as the cat opened his mouth and hissed. Thomas felt his own fur stand up straight on his back, his ears flattened automatically and the sound that escaped his own mouth was foreign. Instinct was now in control, and Thomas acted on its silent commands. The piece of chicken lay forgotten in the dirt as the two cats lowered their heads and howled, each determined to howl louder than the other.

They edged toward each other in an almost ritualistic dance of slow motion. The street cat stood eyeball to eyeball with Thomas, and then very carefully, very slowly, he began to turn ever so tediously, lifting one foot at a time with elaborate care as he retreated, a victim of his own fear of the unfamiliar. Thomas was the first odd-eyed cat the old tom had ever seen.

Thomas returned to his chicken and ate with gusto. *Breeding shows,* he told himself smugly. He was Thomas Bradford, a prince among cats, and these alley bums had just better believe it.

Thomas polished off the bones daintily, washed his face and paws and trotted around to the front street. Once back to the Martin's neighborhood, he would head north. Thomas was convinced this was where he had made his mistake the first time, turning south towards the city instead of north.

The Martins' neighborhood was not as classy as the Bradfords' and the downward trend continued into the city itself, so it was common sense, he reasoned, to look for the Bradfords to the north.

The hot sun beat down on Thomas's back as he hurried along, trying to avoid the cement pavement which seared the pads of his feet. Thomas had no way of knowing it, of course, but today was a special day in his life. It was his birthday, the beginning of his life as an adult cat.

He sniffed the air and broke into a run. Unless his nose was deceiving him, Thomas was on the right track. Faster and faster he ran, and as he did, the scent grew stronger. Thomas was in the Martins' neighborhood, he was sure.

A shrill voice pierced the air, and Thomas quickly ducked behind a bush.

"I'm pushing it."

"Oh, you never let anybody else have a turn."

Two little girls paraded down the street behind a doll carriage and one of them was Courtney Martin.

"It's my turn. You said I could have a turn."

"Let go," Courtney screamed.

They stopped in the middle of the sidewalk right in front of the bush where Thomas hid.

"I hate you, Courtney Martin. You're a mean girl, and I'm not playing with you anymore."

"Don't. See if I care. BABY."

"DUMMY."

"BABY."

"You're the BABY."

"UGLY. Mary Frances is ugly—Mary Frances is ugly."

"I am not, Courtney. I'm gonna tell my mother on you."

"Who cares? Your old mother's ugly, too."

"You're a liar, Courtney."

Mary Frances shoved Courtney. Courtney shoved Mary Frances. Thomas couldn't believe his eyes.

"You're shaking the carriage. You're going to wake up Shirley." Courtney screamed and pulled the other girl's hair.

Something jumped out of the carriage, trailing a blanket. It was a dog—a French Poodle, and it wore a dress and had a pink bow on its head.

Thomas was helpless with suppressed laughter.

"Now look what you did."

"Good. I hope it never comes back."

"Well, you just go and catch it."

"I will not."

"Oh, yes you will, too. That dog cost a lot of money. My daddy said so."

"Your daddy's a BIG BAG OF WIND."

"OH—OW—OH."

They were rolling on the grass, scratching and pulling each other's hair and while they were thus engaged, Thomas slipped out from under the bush. He ran all the way up the street and when he was out of their sight, he sprawled on the ground and rolled and rolled and laughed and laughed.

11

Almost Home

He had been right, Thomas told himself proudly. The farther north he traveled, the nicer the neighborhoods appeared. The houses in Courtney's neightborhood were old, some in need of paint and closer together than those he was approaching.

Here, most of the houses were made of brick or stone instead of wood, and the cars parked in the driveways were newer and shinier, too. Thomas recalled Mr. Martin's car with disgust.

Thomas was a seasoned traveler now, and he had learned to pace himself. He traveled an almost equal distance each day, stopping to nap under a bush when the noonday sun was hottest.

"Oh, look at the white cat. Here, pus."

Thomas saw two old ladies peering at him from behind a hedge.

"Here kitty, kitty, kitty," they called.

Thomas had found old ladies to be harmless, so he entered their yard and allowed them to pet him.

"Go get some milk, Sister," the taller one ordered, and the other lady—who was short and quite fat—hurried into the house, taking mincing little steps on feet which appeared almost too tiny to support her considerable weight.

The tall lady stroked Thomas, rubbing him under the chin the way Marcy used to do. Thomas looked up at her and was startled to see the white hair and wrinkled face, for the gesture had reminded him so much of Marcy.

"Here we are, kitty." The little fat lady put down a big bowl of milk for Thomas to drink.

He lapped it up eagerly. It had been a long time since Thomas had tasted anything so sweet.

"Look, Sister, he was thirsty," the fat lady said.

"He may be lost," the tall one commented.

"Oh dear. If no one comes looking for him, can we keep him?" Sister Fat asked.

Sister Fat and Sister Tall, as Thomas now thought of them, decided to bring Thomas into the house, and if no one claimed him, they would keep him. Thomas figured a short stay with the two old ladies would be a welcome respite from jogging the hot pavements and raiding garbage cans, so he followed them docilely into the house.

"Go get Fluff-Fluff's basket," Sister Tall ordered and again, Sister Fat hurried on little fat feet to the basement. Thomas stood in the kitchen and pondered the identity of Fluff-Fluff. He hadn't smelled another cat, or even a dog in the house.

Sister Fat returned carrying a round, wicker basket which Thomas recognized as some manufacturer's idea of a pet bed. She sat it down on the floor and said, "See kitty, see the nice bed."

The basket contained a blue satin pillow and Thomas sniffed it expertly. Fluff-Fluff was a cat, and Thomas resigned himself to sharing the house with a prima-cat again.

Fluff-Fluff however, did not put in an appearance, and Thomas later gleaned from listening to the two old ladies talk that Fluff-Fluff was deceased. *So much for that,* he thought and settled down on Fluff-Fluff's soft pillow for a nice nap.

Thomas stayed one month and would have stayed longer, if he hadn't overheard a conversation between the sisters and their nephew, Tyson, a frequent visitor to the house.

Tyson called Sister Fat, Aunt Birdie and Sister Tall, Aunt May. He was their bachelor nephew and a music teacher. Tyson came every Thursday for dinner and to spend the evening with his aunts.

He was a portly little man who resembled Sister Fat more than Sister Tall. He wore spectacles, dark suits and a toupee. Thomas judged him to be six or seven years old in cat years.

Thomas usually slept right through Tyson's visits, the conversation being conducive to sleep, and he began to doze now as they spoke.

Tyson was telling the aunts that he had been transferred to a new school and that he would be forced to move, because he always chose to live within walking distance of his schools.

The aunts lamented that nice accomodations were hard to find these days and it was too bad that Tyson would have to give up his present apartment.

It was all very boring, and Thomas couldn't help comparing it to the lively talk that went on at the Collins' house. There one never knew what to expect from the Blue Lady or Marcy. Thomas even thought with nostalgia of the Sir Percival stories. He could do with a little blood and thunder now to keep him awake.

74

Suddenly Thomas sat bolt upright on the pillow. His subconscious mind had picked up something very startling in the conversation. He listened then attentively, wide awake and alert...

He was getting a headache from paying such strict attention to the tedious conversation. What could it have been? And then Tyson repeated, "I shall miss Glenwood Elementary."

Of course, Thomas thought, *Glenwood Elementary is Mark and Judy Bradford's school. And, if Tyson teaches at Glenwood and lives near the school, then it simply follows that Tyson lives near the Bradfords.*

Thomas was elated. He would be home this very night.

♋   ♋   ♋

Thomas sat on the floor of Tyson's car. It had been so easy. He suspected neither Tyson nor his aunts could see too well, even when all three of them wore their glasses.

Nobody had seen him leave the house with Tyson and slip into the car, and his disappearance would probably not be discovered until morning. Then the sisters would become upset, and they'd search the house for him. Sister Tall would have poor Sister Fat breathless, running from cellar to attic, but it would all be in vain.

That's the way the ball bounces, Thomas thought. They'd soon find another cat better suited to them anyway. They were nice old ladies, but they certainly couldn't aspire to owning Thomas Bradford.

Tyson was a slow, cautious driver. Now that Thomas knew his quest was almost at an end, he was anxious to get

75

home. *Almost,* he thought. No, he didn't like that word and wouldn't apply it to himself.

He corrected his thoughts. His quest HAD ended, and he wished he could do something to hurry Tyson along.

They turned into a driveway and Thomas could hardly wait for Tyson to open the door. When he did, Thomas slipped out through his legs.

Tyson said, "Oh, my word," but Thomas never stopped to identify himself.

It was dark and Thomas dodged under a hedge to get his bearings. Across the street, the Glenwood Elementary School stood like a lighthouse to Thomas, the wanderer. Somewhere on its perimeter, the one house Thomas sought was waiting for him.

An hour later Thomas stood on a hill looking down. The house appeared smaller than he had remembered it. He had found it surprisingly fast. It was directly behind the school's athletic field, and the rolling hill that Thomas had glimpsed so many times from the bay window was actually a part of the campus. The house was in darkness, and Thomas supposed it must be very late. *If only old Tyson had driven faster,* he thought.

Thomas ran down the hill and took the fence in one leap. He would sleep on the porch and surprise the family in the morning. He purred in contentment, never dreaming he would not be welcome.

12

The Witch And Gucci Shoes

Thomas woke up with a start. He was drowning in icy water. *This must be a tidal wave,* he thought. He was soaked to the skin and he shook his head to clear his ears and nose when another wave hit him, knocking him down.

"SCAT—GET OUT!"

A woman with a broom was charging toward him and Thomas dove to the ground in terror.

He had caught just a glimpse of the broom wielder, but she was a stranger. Who could she be? And what would such a ferocious person be doing on the Bradford's porch? Thomas took refuge in the hedge where he crouched, shivering, his mind a mass of confusion.

He had been dreaming before his rude awakening and he tried to reconstruct the dream. He had been on a ship, and he hadn't been a cat at all. He had been a man. There was a terrible storm, and he had been clinging to the deckrail to keep from going overbord when the bucket of water had shattered the dream and brought him rudely back to reality. No wonder he had thought it a tidal wave.

So much for strange dreams, Thomas thought. His present predicament was trouble enough. He was in misery from the soaking he had received. A thousand prickles assaulted his body, and the coolness of the morning air only added to his discomfort. He would have to thoroughly brush himself with his rough tongue to dry his fur. He wanted to appear handsome and at his best for the reunion with the family.

The old witch wasn't satisfied with one bucket, she had to drench him with two. *Marcy will give her a piece of her mind,* he thought and then realized that Marcy was far away and out of his life forever. Now, why had he thought of Marcy?

He slunk away, mortified lest anyone should see him in his present condition. Thomas found a secluded spot and there he went to work trying to restore his soaked fur. His mother's words came back to him. "Never get your fur wet. It is very bad for the coat-takes away all the natural oils."

Thomas's little tongue was sore when he had finished cleaning, but his coat glowed, its silky softness restored. He stretched out on the grass to let the sun finish the job. He was proud of his appearance. There wasn't a mark on him to mar the perfection of his whiteness. He had paid special attention to his paws, remembering Queenie's meticulous obsession with paws. His were now as pink as the day he was born.

He was reluctant to go back to the house and have the witch douse him with water again, so he decided to wait until Mark and Judy came home from school. He lounged around for the better part of the day and when he saw the sun was in its afternoon position, he sauntered back.

Thomas waited behind a large bush, but Mark and Judy did not appear. Lots of other boys and girls walked past though, and Thomas was growing impatient for the long-awaited reunion.

When no more children passed carrying books, Thomas decided he must have missed them. Now he would have to wait for Charlie Bradford to come home from work.

He took a nap and presently an expensive looking black automobile turned into the driveway. *Charlie Bradford must have gotten a new car,* Thomas thought. It certainly was classy looking, but then nothing but the best would be sufficient for the Bradfords. Thomas thought of Mr. Martin's run-down car again and smiled to himself.

He ran to the kitchen door. He'd sneak in with Charlie and surprise the whole family.

Long legs encased in grey flannel trousers almost succeeded in crowding Thomas off the step while the man fumbled with the door key. Thomas smiled again. Charlie Bradford hadn't even noticed him.

The door opened and Thomas was suddenly propelled into the kitchen on the toe of a Gucci boot. Long grey flannel legs flailed the air in a vain attempt to keep the Gucci shoes firmly on the floor, as the big man fell with a loud crash. Thomas, the cause of it all, dived under the kitchen table.

"What happened?" a woman's voice screamed.

"I tripped over something. I think it was a cat," the man moaned.

Thomas could only see the woman's feet, but he was eye to eye with the man now and it wasn't Charlie Bradford lying on the floor.

Thomas looked from the man up to the woman and then once quickly around the room. *Who are these people, and what had happened to the Bradfords' kitchen?*

The maple kitchen table was gone, replaced by a smoked glass monstrosity with wrought iron legs. Instead of the four sturdy wooden chairs, there were now only two chairs, wrought iron like the table and cushioned with green velvet.

The Cat of the Month calendar was gone from the wall. In its place was the ugliest picture Thomas ever seen—just blotches of color splashed all over a canvas and framed.

"GET THAT CAT —THAT CAT! It's in the house," the woman screamed and Thomas recognized her as the witch who'd thrown water on him. "GET THE BROOM!" she yelled and Thomas ran into the dining room.

The dining room was as distorted as the kitchen—all the Bradfords' furniture was gone and the witch's furniture was in its place. *Did she changed the Bradfords into something else, too?* Thomas knew witches could do those things. They could turn princes into frogs and vice versa. Judy Bradford had a book on it.

Thomas crawled under a china closet and peered out. He saw the witch's feet enter the room. "Come in here and help me find it," she yelled to the man.

He sounded like he was still out of breath from his earlier gymnastics. "Just open the door, and it'll go outside."

The witch grabbed a broom and suddenly Thomas was terrified. He had heard about witches and their brooms, too. They rode in the air on them, so they had to be magic. If she touched him with it, would he turn into something else? Or worse still, just disappear—evaporate into thin air, all of his nine lives wiped out in one sweep.

Thomas shot out from under the china cabinet and headed in the direction of the kitchen again. The man was standing by the sink drinking a glass of water. When he saw Thomas

80

streak into the room, he made a beeline for the door, throwing it open wide, and Thomas raced outside.

He never stopped running until he had reached the top of the hill.

13

Water, Water, Everywhere

Water stretched before him, behind him and all about him—an endless sea of deep blue. He appeared to be the only living creature above the sea. It was the loneliest, the most forsaken feeling he had ever known.

Where were the others? Had none been spared save him? He was in a small lifeboat, but there were no oars and so he drifted, a prisoner of the sea, subject to her whims—this way, that way, an insignificant speck on her vast and ageless bosom.

He cupped his hands around his lips and called out, "AHOY—AHOY," but his ears alone recorded the sound. He stared down into the depths which would surely become his final resting place, and he was almost tempted to embrace his conqueror, to fling himself into her warmth, and cheat her of her torture. But something held him back—something within himself that would not believe he could end this way.

He looked at his hands, strong, young hands tanned to golden brown, hardened and calloused from months at sea. He studied his arms. Strong muscles rippled under the smooth brown flesh, and the hairs were bleached to palest blond.

He was young. He was invincible. He shook his fist at the cruel sea and raised his head high to see an atoll in the distance. He thrust his hands into the water and used them as paddles. He would make it. He had no doubt.

♋   ♋   ♋

Thomas awoke with a start. He was on the hillside overlooking the athletic field, and all about him was green grass. To the right of him stretched the ball field, deserted now. No click of ball meeting bat, or smack of ball meeting glove broke the silence of the twilight. The playground, too, was deserted, and the vacant swings moved slightly and eerily in the autumn wind. Lights had been turned on in the houses at the foot of the hill.

It was that time of evening when all creatures were home. For Thomas, there was no home. Fate had set him adrift, to be tossed this way and that way without compass or direction. He had never felt so alone.

He looked down at his paws, manicured to perfection for Queenie's benefit. Where was she now, his gentle, beautiful mother?

He felt stiff and he stretched. Vague and distorted patches of a dream jogged his memory. He had been a man again in the dream, but the rest was just a blur. He yawned, filling his lungs with the cool, fresh air. He was alive and young.

Suddenly his spirits lifted. He held his tail high and walked down the hill. He would find his father. He was a king's son, and he had many lives to live.

14

Long Live The King

The neighborhood strays were not receptive to a newcomer, and it was several days before Thomas met an old rover nicknamed Hungry Joe who gave him the facts.

The Bradfords had not been turned into frogs; neither was the water-douser a witch. The truth was, the Bradfords had moved and sold their house to the Broom-Wielder and Gucci Shoes. The new owners hated cats, dogs, bugs, mice, children, dirt and noise in that order, according to Hungry Joe, who seemed to know everything about everybody.

Hungry Joe was the most disreputable looking cat Thomas had ever seen. He was a striped tabby with a huge head and sad, golden eyes. His left ear had a piece chewed out, one of many battle scars Hungry would carry to his grave. In spite of his rakish appearance, though, there was a dignity about Hungry, and Thomas liked him from the start.

He was a wealth of information to Thomas. He had watched the Bradfords move. A huge truck had taken all the furniture away and then the Bradfords had come out with suitcases and boxes and piled into the station wagon. Queenie was in a cat case, and Judy was holding it. They had moved to a place called Florida, and it was far away.

Thomas was undaunted. He would get to Florida somehow, but first he'd have a reunion with his father. Could Hungry Joe take Thomas to Big Tom?

"I was afraid you'd ask that," Hungry said and his sad yellow eyes looked sadder than ever. He was a good hearted cat, and he hated to have to tell this fine young aristocrat that he'd not only lost a home and mother, but his father as well.

"It happened about six months ago," Hungry said. "Big Tom was hit by a truck—killed instantly, he was. He didn't suffer, and that should be a comfort to you."

Thomas was shocked. He hadn't known his father, but Big Tom, king of the alley cats had been indestructible in Thomas's mind.

Suddenly he was back in Marcy's office and he heard: *Sir Percival said, 'The king is dead.' The young prince was brought to the throne room and the heavy crown was placed on the boy's head. LONG LIVE THE KING, the people shouted.*

Was Thomas now a king?

"What will you do now?" Hungry asked.

Thomas answered him mechanically, "Go to Florida and search again."

"Could I go with you? I'd like a change of scene, and I'll help you."

Marcy's voice spoke to Thomas again: *The crown weighed heavy on the young king's head. 'Too much, too soon,' Sir Percival said. 'Even a king hath need of a friend.'*

"Yes, you may go if you've a mind to," Thomas answered grandly, and they marched down the street, Thomas walking just a little ahead of Hungry Joe.

15

Danger Ahead

They worked well together. Hungry was a good foil for Thomas. His tabby coat was a veritable camouflage where Thomas's whiteness could not be concealed.

Their favorite and most successful heists were accomplished in delicatessens or small meat markets. Thomas would boldly enter the store, jump up on the counter, and while the proprietor would be busy chasing Thomas out the door, Hungry would have selected the loot and made off with it. Then they would meet, usually around the corner, to share the feast.

They went back to the old neighborhood just once for a bit of devilment. Thomas hadn't forgotten the indignity he had suffered from the Water-Douser, alias the Witch; so they collected a dozen good-sized dead mice and deposited them at the kitchen door. Then, just for good measure, they walked all over Gucci Shoes' Lincoln Continental, leaving countless paw prints on the shiny black hood.

"That'll teach them a lesson," Thomas said to Hungry as they ran side by side, leaving the Glenwood community behind them forever.

Hungry had heard there was a train heading south, and he and Thomas planned to be on it.

The weather was turning cold, and Thomas noticed that the houses had trees in them hung with silver and gold ornaments. That reminded him of Marcy and the Christmas he had spent with the Collins family. He wondered what they were doing and whether they still missed him.

A feeling of longing washed over him, but he shook it off. He was on his way to Florida to take his rightful place. He was now a king. Long live the king.

Over fences and under cars, they raced through suburbia like long distance runners. Passersby could hardly distinguish them as cats, so swiftly did they fly.

Hungry knew the city like his own paw, and Thomas marveled at his new friend. For one of questionable ancestry, Hungry displayed considerable intelligence and cunning.

When they arrived at the railyard it was dusk.

"A good time for concealment," Hungry said and then looked quizzically at Thomas. "Might I offer a suggestion?" he asked politely.

"I'm always ready to listen," Thomas answered. "Which is not to say I'll always agree."

Thomas remembered a line from *Sir Percival's Revenge, 'Tis a foolish king who closes his ears to counsel, for even out of the mouths of idiots great truths sometimes flow. Consider ye well thy subject's petitions. Ye are no less sovereign for it. Verily I say, even a cat may gaze at a king.*

"Your coat is magnificent," Hungry said. "But I fear it'll be our downfall. You're just too white to hide in a boxcar." When Thomas nodded, Hungry was emboldened to continue. "Now, if you were to disguise yourself..." Hungry paused for effect and then jerked his head to the right. "That load of coal might just do the trick," he added quickly, not sure of the little king's reaction to such sacrilege.

Thomas, however, was more practical than vain, and in one leap he was on top of the coal car. When he emerged, he was a dusty grey color. Even Hungry would not have recognized him at first glance.

Thomas wondered how they should know which train to take, but he dared not show his ignorance before Hungry Joe.

"This way," Hungry called, and Thomas followed him away from the tracks and down a hillside.

Two men sat huddled around a weak fire. Both of them wore shabby, ill-fitting clothes and one of them had a cough which made him sound like a barking dog.

"You pullin' out tonight?" the cougher asked between barks.

"Yup."

"Where to?"

"Boston."

The cougher was overcome at this point, and the bark turned to a wheeze that wracked his thin body. The other man pounded him on the back, and the coughing subsided enough to allow him to speak. "I'm headin' for Florida where it's warm. I don't ever wanna be cold again. Be leavin' in a few minutes."

"Good luck to ya," the other said, and Hungry looked knowingly at Thomas.

Thomas understood. Hungry might be ugly, but he sure wasn't dumb. They followed the Florida-bound hobo and were right behind him when he climbed aboard the train.

It was a huge boxcar jammed with crates and boxes of every size and description. Thomas and Hungry slipped past the hobo and moved to the opposite side of the car.

This was a new experience for Thomas. He had ridden in cars, but these things they called trains were something else. They reminded Thomas of giant black snakes and when the door clanged shut and the thing began to slither along the track in total darkness, Thomas felt his back prickle with a strong premonition of terrible danger.

16

Of Dreams And Friends

He felt like he was coming out of a long, dark tunnel. The light at the end was bright and it hurt his eyes. He opened them cautiously. He saw blue skies and he heard the gentle lapping of waves meeting the shore.

He was lying on a deserted beach. His muscles were stiff, but he felt no pain. Sitting up, he inspected his body— no wounds, nothing broken. He dug his toes into the sand, relishing the feel of it, the warm, soft sand sliding over his bare feet.

The sun had dried his water-soaked clothes and stuck them to his body. How long had he lain here? He looked out toward the sea. The tide was low, and it exposed jagged rocks all along the shoreline. How had he maneuvered the boat past them? It was beached not a yard away from him, he noticed.

He stood up, turning his back on the sea and looked toward the island. He was struck by its beauty. Beyond the white beach dotted with palms lay lush vegetation. He saw what looked like mango trees full of fruit and bushes covered with berries. He was suddenly hungry, and he ran to stuff his mouth with the luscious, red fruit.

It was sublime. *This is a paradise,* he told himself, *a tiny, tropical jewel, but why hasn't it been developed?* Still eating, he climbed expertly up the mango tree for a better view of the island. He could see clear to the other side, also undeveloped. He shouted, "AHOY, AHOY," but only the birds answered his call.

Tossing down several ripe mangos, he shinnied down the tree. Breaking open the fruit, he ate, but they were not mangos, he decided. Like the berries, this was something he had never tasted before. It was delicious, and he cracked the second one open eagerly. It looked completely different from the first! Puzzled, he bit cautiously into the fruit. It was nothing like the first! *How can this be?* he asked himself.

A feeling of panic seized him, and he tore the third fruit apart to find that it was yet another species, distinctly and completely different from both of the others.

This is impossible, he thought. *No tree on earth produces a variety of fruit.*

"No tree on EARTH!" he said aloud. Where was he?

He looked toward the sea again and at the treacherous rocks which guarded its shoreline. No one on earth could maneuver a wooden rowboat through those waters. How did he, a novice sailor, using his bare hands for oars, make it here?

"Where am I?" he shouted, running along the beach in panic. He felt the soft sand on his feet. He felt the coldness of the water as a playful wave rushed up and caught him unawares. The sun felt hot on his back. He stopped suddenly and again spoke aloud. "I can feel, I can see and hear. I can't be dead. There has to be a rational explanation for all of this."

"AHOY, AHOY." The sound caught him off-guard. He stood up and looked toward the island. Was it his imagination? Was it an echo of his own voice? Had his words circled the island and come back now to taunt him with an empty hope?

"AHOY—AHOY."

He followed the sound. Up there on the ridge he spotted a man. He was not alone! Sudden tears filled his eyes and he ran toward the figure poised above him. "AHOY," he shouted in answer.

The man saw him and started down the cliff. As he drew closer, he saw that the stranger was about his own age, a small, swarthy man with moderately long hair and a large black mustache. He wore cut-off black trousers and a full-sleeved shirt. He looked Latin.

Groping for words, vaguely remembered from sophomore Spanish, he addressed him, "Bueños dios, Señor."

"Heaven be praised. My prayers are answered," the other said in perfect English. Embracing him, he added, "Ah, my friend, you don't know how happy I am to see another man like myself."

The sheer joy of finding human companionship overwhelmed them both, and tears misted their eyes.

"I am José Juan Manuel DeCosta, from Madrid," the stranger said proudly. Then he clicked his heels and bowed elaborately in a gesture straight out of a period movie.

Joining in the game, the tall, blond American bowed low, too and said, "And I am Dashiell David Collins, from America."

♋ ♋ ♋

Thomas opened his eyes to the inky darkness of the enclosed car as the train rumbled through the night. Hungry was curled up tightly, his paws tucked under his body for warmth as he slept.

That dream again. What did it mean? Now Thomas knew who he was in the dream—Dash Collins. How strange that he should dream he was Dash. Or was it really strange? From the very first hadn't Thomas felt himself drawn to the handsome young man? Hadn't he even been aware of a strange fact—that had he been a man, Thomas would have been Dash Collins? Tall, silver haired and god-like, a king among men, Dash Collins was Thomas Bradford's alter ego. Or, was it the other way around?

Thomas wondered where Dash Collins was now and what he had done since storming out of his parents' home.

"It's sure cold in this place," Hungry remarked and Thomas was glad his friend was awake. The dream had unnerved him, given him a heavy feeling of impending doom. Was the feeling for himself, for Dash, or for them both?

"How long will we be in this thing? Thomas asked Hungry, anxious to turn to mundane matters.

"We should be in North Carolina in the morning," Hungry answered. "The train will have to unload and then reload there."

"Hungry, how do you know all these things?" Thomas asked, curiosity overcoming his pride.

"I've traveled before. I was born in a freight yard. We never had a home," Hungry added. "I've been on my own since I was about four weeks old. My mother was killed by some humans in the yard."

"Killed—how?"

"They poured gasoline on her and set her on fire. They thought it was a good joke."

"Oh, Hungry, I'm sorry." Thomas sighed. "I wouldn't have asked if..."

"It's all right. I can talk about it now, but for a long time, well, you know, I was just a kitten, and for a long time I wouldn't have anything to do with humans. I thought they were all the same, but then I found out, there's good and bad in everything. I've met some cats in my travels who've had homes and got lost, you know. Gee, they had it so good." Hungry's ugly face took on a wistful look. "How come you left all them good homes you had, Thomas?"

Thomas felt a reprimand in Hungry's question. "Now you know I'm going to Florida to find the Bradfords. You don't think I'd stay with the Martins and be called, 'Shirley,' do you? Or live with two old ladies where the highlight of the week is watching 'The Lawrence Welk Show?'"

"I didn't mean the Martins, but—well, old ladies ain't so bad. They were good to you, you said."

"Of course, but they weren't my type."

"Well, what about the other people—the lady what wrote the books about Sir Whatsisname?"

"Sir Percival."

"Oh yeah. Sir Percival and the lady's mama. What color lady was she?"

"THE BLUE LADY, THE BLUE LADY," Thomas shouted with impatience. "Can't you get anything right, Hungry? I told you they were not extraordinary people."

"Oh, I see."

"No, you don't see," Thomas snapped, tucking his paws under him and closing his eyes to discourage Hungry from any more talk. He made Thomas feel guilty. He was sorry about Hungry's mother, but why did he have to bring up the Collins' family? They *were* good people, the best, but Thomas Bradford was a king, and a king had to surround himself with extraordinary people, didn't he?

17

In The Hands Of
The Enemy

"We're slowing down," Thomas said.

"That means we're coming into a station," Hungry murmured, still half asleep.

"Don't we have to hide? Won't they be opening the car?"

"We've plenty of time," Hungry explained importantly. Thomas Bradford might be a king, but Hungry knew his trains. "I'll let you know when to hide."

Thomas hated the dirty, black things. He'd be glad when they arrived in Florida, and he could take a good bath. He looked down at his fur. It was a disgrace. The grime and soot that he had rolled in on the coal car mixed with grease picked up in the boxcar, and Thomas was a mess.

Hungry's tabby coat was unchanged. There was something to be said for a mixture such as Hungry's.

"How long will we lay over?" Thomas asked.

"About an hour. They unload the boxes for North Carolina and then add more shipments heading for Florida. This is where we have to be careful, Thomas. Some of these men are pretty rough and they would think nothing of doing us in—shooting us or burning us."

Hungry's reference to his mother's horrible death touched Thomas. "Don't worry, Hungry. We'll outwit them. After all, we do have nine lives, you know."

"You might have nine left. You're still young, but I musta used up a heap of mine over the past six years."

"Well, come to think of it, I guess I've used one or two myself."

Hungry's ears stood up straight. "NOW," he said. "Look for a good hiding place."

Both cats scrambled to the back of the car. Hungry squeezed himself between two large crates, and Thomas moved against the wall of the boxcar. He could see absolutely nothing, but after an eternity, he heard the heavy steel door being pulled back and then voices:

"Man—Lookit this here mess. What idiot loaded this car? Gimmie a hand here, Luke."

"Ah hate these Florida cars, always loaded to the hilt. Shove that box over here, Sonny."

Thomas could hear the scraping of boxes being shoved across the floor of the car. He hoped they'd soon finish. He didn't like their voices. They reminded him of Roy Johnson and his pal who'd tried to shoot him out of a tree.

"Hey Sonny—come here. We gotta stiff on this here train."

"Well, I'll be. He's daid all right."

"I'll go git somebody."

"No. Wait."

"What fer?"

"He might have some money on him. These hobos'll fool ya. Close that door, Luke."

97

Thomas could hear the heavy door being pulled shut, and then the car was in darkness once again.

"Set that flashlight up there on a box, so's we can see."

"You sure he's daid, Sonny? We might git in some trouble."

"Shut up and help me. What trouble, ya big dummy? Hey, looka here, twenty dollars. Check his other pocket."

"Nothin."

"So, ten fer me and ten fer you. Ain't bad. I'll bet he had a bottle though. These winos always bring their bottles."

"We don't need no bottle, Sonny. We better report this."

"Flash that light around. What the—I seen a cat. Gimmie that flashlight, Luke."

The flashlight caught Thomas on the back of the head and knocked him out.

"I knowed that was a cat."

"We don't need no cat, Sonny. Let's git goin and report the stiff."

"Shut up, Luke. Gimmie that sack."

"Whatcha gonna do?"

"Gonna stuff this here cat in the sack, dummy. I kin git another ten spot fer it."

"Ten dollars! Nobody gonna give you ten dollars for no mangy old cat, Sonny."

"That's what you think. This ole cat gonna buy us a ticket to a fight. You ever hear tell of a pit fight, Luke?"

With teeth bared, Hungry shot out from behind a box and attacked Sonny. He clawed and bit at the hand that held the sack.

Sonny screamed in pain and Luke backed off from the snarling, ferocious looking cat.

"Git him off me. Git him off me."

"He's wild, Sonny. He's..."

"Hand me that flaslight, ya fool."

Sonny brought the flashlight down on Hungry's head, and the needle sharp teeth and claws were released from his arm. Sonny wiped the blood from his hand and said, "Put it in the sack. Or, are ya afraid it might bite ya now?"

"I ain't afraid. I jest..."

"Ah shut up and go make the report. First though, take this sack and put it in ma truck."

♋ ♋ ♋

Thomas regained consciousness first. He opened his eyes to find himself in a heavy, burlap sack with Hungry beside him. Thomas looked at his friend. Hungry was breathing, but he had a nasty knot on the top of his head. Thomas licked the wound, and Hungry whimpered.

"Hold still and let me sterilize it," Thomas told him.

Hungry opened his eyes. "Is it a big bump?"

"Big as a robin's egg."

"It's a good thing I've got a hard head. He really whammed me," Hungry said.

"He must have hit me, too. The last thing I remember is something flying through the air towards me."

"He threw the flashlight at you," Hungry told him.

"I guess my hiding place wasn't so good, but how did he find you?"

Hungry modestly refrained from telling Thomas the truth. "I guess my hiding place wasn't so good either."

"Well, that makes me feel better. At least it wasn't my fault we got captured."

"These things just happen sometimes," Hungry said.

"Nonsense. They may happen to ordinary cats, not to kings. But, don't worry, Hungry, I'll think of a way to get us out of it," Thomas said importantly. "Put not down thy crown, even for a moment. For a king is a king, is a king. Sir Percival's Revenge, Chapter 10."

"What?" Hungry asked.

"Nothing. Rest yourself. I need to think."

Yes, that's it, Thomas decided. *He forgot who he was, and let Hungry take charge. Now look at the mess they were in. Well, he'd just have to get them out of it.*

Thomas began to tear at the burlap with his claws. *Surely a king can find his way out of a burlap bag,* he told himself.

They worked together on the bag for what seemed like hours, but neither of them could make a rip in the burlap. Both of their heads throbbed and they licked each other's wounds as best they could.

"What do you think they want with us?" Thomas finally asked Hungry.

"I don't know," Hungry answered, for he hadn't the heart to burden Thomas with his worst fears. Hungry had heard of pit fights, and if his conclusions were correct, Thomas would have to be more than a king to get them out of this.

18

Lost In Paradise

Dash looked at his new friend. "How long have you been on this island?" he asked.

"I've lost track of time, but I think about six months."

"Where did your ship go down?"

Dash was completely disoriented, but maybe between the two of them, they could ascertain how far they were from civilization.

"Off Cape Hattaras."

"Mine, too. Where were you bound?"

"Back to Spain. We had a rich cargo, too—probably all in the hands of buccaneers now."

Dash laughed at the other's attempt at humor, but José looked at him strangely and continued talking.

"I've been a seaman since I turned sixteen, and I never did see a storm to equal that one."

"I know what you mean. It was the same with us. We were carrying oranges up the coast from Florida. God knows how far we drifted in that hurricane."

Again José regarded Dash quizzically.

"I'm not really a seaman," Dash explained. "I just took the job because the pay was good. I hope to go back to Harvard next year."

José made no comment. "There are natives on this island," he said, shifting the subject.

Dash was surprised. "That should help. Do they have a radio?"

José looked at Dash blankly.

"You mean they're uncivilized?

"They are natives. They're not unfriendly," José answered. "I've been living at their village, and they've sent up smoke signals, but no ship has passed in all these months."

"How do you communicate with them?"

"Oh, they speak Spanish very well. You'll see. I'll take you to meet them. Only I should warn you, they'll think you're a king. They have a legend—perhaps from the teachings of Christian missionaries. They are waiting for the arrival of a king—a tall white man with golden hair—to redeem them. When they see you, they will be positive you are their god-man. Come, I take you there now."

The village was on the other side of the island. The thatched-roof huts were concentrated in a clearing hardly more than five or six acres in size.

Several young boys spotted the visitors and ran to greet them. When they saw Dash, they prostrated themselves at his feet.

"Tell them to get up. Make them understand I'm not their king," Dash told José.

"It would do no good, my friend. They are primitives. Let them hold to their beliefs. It may be to our advantage."

One of the boys, a lad of about twelve, raised his head and looked at Dash, and Dash was struck by the child's beauty. "Oh, great king," the boy said in perfect English. "You have come."

102

The other two boys, emboldened by their comrade's courage, raised their heads and stole a look at Dash. Then all three ran off, shouting to the elders that the Golden King had come.

What manner of people are these? Dash asked himself. *They speak two foreign languages fluently and yet, by all accounts they have been isolated on a tiny island for centuries. This cannot be. José DeCosta may speak excellent English, but mastering several languages is not an uncommon feat for a seaman of nine or ten years. In other ways though, José appears slow-witted,* Dash thought, recalling the other's blank stares. Dash had an idea that José had never inquired about a radio.

"Is there a chief?" Dash asked José.

"Yes, he's coming out now." José nodded his head toward a very old man, emerging from one of the huts.

The chief's great joy shone in his eyes as he, too, knelt in homage at Dash's feet. Dash was impatient to talk, and as he surveyed the scene of a hundred or more natives with bowed heads and their palm-thatched huts in the background, he couldn't help thinking the whole thing was straight out of an old B movie. At any minute, he half expected to see his grandmother, the young Buela Blue of questionable fame, descend from the sky as the Moon Goddess or some such entity and then a knicker-clad director would call, "CUT."

The unreal scene continued, though, and finally Dash and José were invited into the chief's hut for refreshment and conversation.

They sat in a circle and drank a delicious drink which Dash imagined to be coconut milk. Taking the lead, Dash asked the chief a series of questions designed to make some sense out of this nightmare.

When they had been answered, he was more confused than ever. The island was called "Lananobi." The chief had no idea where it was located. No one had been off the island since the great storm which had washed away a neighboring island and all its inhabitants. Lananobi and all her people had survived, but the chief believed the storm had pushed the island far out to sea and isolated it from the rest of the world.

"Have visitors come to the island since the storm?" Dash asked.

"Only Señor DeCosta and yourself," was the answer.

"What about before the storm?"

Surely, Spanish and English visitors had come and taught the natives to speak the white man's languages, Dash thought.

However, the king insisted, "Speak only Lananobi."

Dash ignored the answer and went on with his questions. When had the great storm occurred? Had it been in the chief's lifetime? Had he witnessed it?

Yes, the chief and all the people living on the island now had witnessed the storm.

"How long ago was it?" Dash persisted.

"Many moons ago." The chief's evasions troubled Dash. *Are these people really as friendly as they seem?* But, the old man's face gave no hint of guile.

Lowering his head, the chief asked in a respectful tone, "Was the storm sent as a punishment for my people?"

Dash assured him that it was not.

"Why then are my people cursed?" the old man asked.

"Cursed? In what way?" Dash inquired.

104

"No child has been born on Lananobi since the great storm. We are a dying people if we cannot renew ourselves with fresh blood."

"Show me the youngest child on the island," Dash said impulsively.

The chief clapped his hands, and immediately a young woman appeared. Dash's request was repeated to her.

"Manu," she said softly, leaving the hut and returning with the boy who had greeted Dash when he entered the village.

"How old is Manu?" Dash asked.

Both the chief and the woman stared blankly at him.

"They have no conception of time," José said under his breath.

The chief turned to Dash. "If this is not punishment for our sins, the devil must have cursed us. Please, great king. You are more powerful. Remove this curse. We have treasure and we humbly offer it to you. Come, great king, let us show you our offerings."

Dash and José exchanged surprised glances, as they followed the chief from the hut.

He led them to a cave on the south side of the island.

"All of this is yours, mighty king. We humbly beg that you favor us by removing the curse."

The chief stood back, allowing them to see into the chamber.

Dash could make no comment, for his senses reeled at the sight.

19

Remember The Good Times

Both Thomas and Hungry had fallen asleep after futile efforts at ripping the bag which held them captive. When they awoke, the truck was moving, and they recognized the voices of Luke and Sonny coming from the front seat.

"How far is it?"

"It ain't how far, its how good it's hid. We gonna git a bumpy ride, Luke boy. From here on out ain't nothin', but dirt roads ahead."

"How you know 'bout this here pit fight, Sonny?"

"Seen it advertised in the paper."

"No kiddin'."

Sonny roared with laughter. "Ya big dummy—it's agin the law. You think they'd put it in the paper? Boy, you sure are dumb. Ah heard 'bout it around the yard, pea brain. Lefty won three hundred bucks last week. We're gonna say Lefty sent us."

"Lefty wouldn't do that, Sonny. Lefty don't like us."

"Shut up. You know that, I know that, and Lefty knows it, but they don't. Lefty ain't even gonna be there tonight, so nobody'll be the wiser. We're gonna give um these two ole cats and—holy cow—they're still alive ain't they?"

Luke reached back and punched the burlap bag, and Thomas dug his claws into Luke's hand. "Ouch. Them cats is wild, Sonny. Ah hope they ain't got no rabies."

106

"What is a pit fight?" Thomas asked, but Hungry pretended to be asleep.

Thomas might be an aristocrat, but he was young, and it was better that he not know. For himself, Hungry was resigned to his fate. His life had been hard from the very beginning. Why should he expect an easy end to it? His heart went out to Thomas though—a fine young king like Thomas should not have to suffer such an ignoble death.

"There it is."

"Where?"

"Over yonder in that abandoned farm house."

"Here comes somebody, Sonny."

Thomas heard a third voice:

"What y'all want? This here private prop'ty."

"He gotta rifle, Sonny—Let's go."

"Shut up. It's OK. Lefty sent us. We got two cats here in a sack."

"Shorty don't want no cats. Shorty uses small dogs for bait."

"But, these cats is wild—no kiddin'. Got me good on the hand—look."

A fourth voice in the distance shouted:

"Who's out there?"

"Two guys. Lefty sent 'em. They got two cats in a sack, but I tole 'em you don't use no cats, Shorty."

The fourth man now joined the others.

"Whatta ya want for them cats?"

"Ten bucks apiece."

"Give ya five each and tickets to the next fight."

107

"When's the fight?"

"Friday night—10 o'clock. Gonna be a good one—two Dobermans. One called Killer's won five fights straight."

"We'll be here. Dobermans! Man o' man, them dawgs is somethin else."

"Ah always was scared of Dobermans. Can't git out, can they?"

"Shut up, Luke, and git them cats outa the back."

The burlap bag was dragged out of the truck, tossing Thomas and Hungry this way and that way. They felt the bag being slung in the air, over someone's shoulder probably, and then it was rudely dropped on the floor.

A hand reached into the sack and Thomas tried to bite it, but these were expert animal handlers. The hand seized Thomas by the back of the neck, and he was brought out, struggling, but helpless.

"Git in there," the man said, shoving Thomas into a small wire cage.

Thomas watched as Hungry was dragged from the sack in the same manner and shoved into another cage.

They were in a barn, Thomas saw, and on the straw-covered floor were five or six small cages. Three were empty, and two contained small dogs, a red Pekingese and a white poodle.

The man wore boots, and that was all of him that Thomas could see from his position on the floor. The odor of his hate was strong and foul, and for the first time since a snowy night long ago outside Marcy's house, Thomas Bradford knew dispair.

When the barn door banged shut and the heavy footsteps grew faint, Hungry spoke. "You all right, Thomas?"

Thomas didn't answer. This latest evidence of human cruelty had caused the young cat to withdraw and turn his face to the wall near the cage.

Hungry knew the feeling. Hadn't he reacted the very same way after witnessing the brutal murder of his mother? But, Hungry knew something else—that bitterness turns inward, poisoning the heart and that this is the enemy's ultimate triumph.

"Thomas, listen to me," Hungry pleaded. "Don't turn your face to the wall. We may get out of this and we may not, but at any rate, we have lived, and there's been good times, lots more for you than for me. Let's talk about the good times, Thomas. You go first. Tell me about when you had a home."

Hungry waited anxiously, hoping against hope for some response, and then he heard: "Some of the best times were early in the morning, just Marcy, Sheba and me. Sheba would sit on the desk. I'd get in the file cabinet and Marcy would turn on her dictaphone. Sunshine would stream through the windows, making the room deliciously warm and Marcy would tell us about Sir Percival. Marcy had a soft, musical voice, and sometimes Sheba and I would both fall asleep listening to her."

20

The Bitter Truth

Dash and José stood in the cave's chamber. The room, approximately twelve feet on each side, was filled with gold and silver coins overflowing their casks.

The chief had left them alone to examine the treasure—his people's offering to the Golden King.

"There's a fortune in Spanish gold here," Dash said, gazing in awe at the wealth before them. "Taken from some old sunken ship," he murmured to himself.

"From our ship," José said stiffly.

"Your ship? José, look. These are pieces of eight. These coins must be over two hundred years old."

"No, from our ship," José insisted in a strange voice. "We were carrying gold and silver from Mexico. We met four of my country's galleons in Havana. We must travel in convoy because you British do not respect treaties."

"José, I'm not British," Dash said kindly. "I'm American."

"You mean you're a colonist."

Dash nodded. It would be useless and maybe even dangerous to contradict him. *I should have known,* he thought. *So many signs and yet I didn't see his instability.*

José ran his hands through his thick black hair. "I'm sorry," he said. "I'm not myself. Seeing this evidence from my ship has upset me. Where are my mates? Where is my ship?"

Suddenly José stood up and looked around. "Why have I never seen this cave before? I've been on this island for months and combed it completely. Why did I not find this place? I must find my ship," he added in a confused voice and ran from the chamber.

Dash sat and thought about this latest turn of events. *A Spanish galleon must have been shipwrecked on this island more than two hundred years ago, and the natives stored the treasure through generations, waiting for the arrival of their king. That made sense. As to the curse of the unborn babies, some disease could have afflicted the islanders, leaving them sterile.*

What a pity about José though, a likeable little guy, but the shipwreck and the loneliness must have been too much for him. He'd better find him and calm him down, Dash decided.

As he came out of the cave, José ran towards him, "Come and see." His eyes glittered with excitement, and he grabbed Dash by the arm, pulling him with maniacal strength down an embankment. "Hurry," he cried impatiently, leading Dash through a forest thick with ferns.

Abruptly the forest ended and opened onto a small cove. "Look," José said, and Dash found himself gazing at a double masted galleon, her sails moving eerily in the wind.

It's a mirage, he thought, *a ghost ship*. He'd heard of such, but he allowed himself to be pulled closer and closer by José until they were both in the water swimming the short distance out to the ship, which rested on a sandbar.

As they climbed aboard, Dash saw the name, still legible on the hull, *Marguerita*. This is some kind of joke. José must have found the ship before, but José was already below deck, calling, "Juan, Pedro, Capitan..."

Dash looked around him. The ship was clean. *Shouldn't it have been covered with barnacles, its deck rotted and mildewed? Is José crazy or am I?* he wondered.

"They are all gone, disappeared." José stood before Dash, tears streaming down his cheeks. "Here is the log."

Dash looked at the last entry. "This is in English," he said, but José shook his head vigorously.

"No, no, Spanish. Read."

More confused than ever, Dash returned to the log and read: "December 5, 1650—The storm is gaining fury. There is a terrible blue lightening, and the sailors are much afraid. We are in the Devil's Sea."

The Sargasso Sea, Dash thought. They called it the Devil's Sea—the most treacherous stretch of the Bermuda Triangle. Now he knew, and the truth boggled the mind. José had gone down in the Bermuda Triangle, and so had he. Where were they now? He looked at José, weeping for his lost comrades. Poor José, a man plucked from the 17th century and dropped into the 20th. Or was it the other way around? Had he, Dash Collins, been swept backwards in time to the sixteen hundreds? It was too fantastic to comprehend. He had read of time warps, and he tried to remember what he had read.

"Forgive me, my friend, for what I said in the cave. Our countries might be enemies, but we can be friends. Please Dash, I need your friendship," José said softly.

Dash put his hand on José's shoulder. "And I need your friendship, too, José—more than you know."

What was he to do? He could never confide his suspicions to José. How could he tell this man from another time that it was he who was lost and not his comrades? They rested in peace at the bottom of the sea, but José resided in a twilight zone—neither alive nor dead, a perfectly preserved relic, doomed perhaps to remain forever in this half-life state, as he himself was doomed. The great Dash Collins, destined for such heights of glory, or so he had thought, was now stuck for all time as king of the island of Lananobi.

Time passed, or Dash supposed it passed. How could time be measured in a place like this? José had thought himself marooned for six months when in fact it had been three hundred years. Dash lay on the beach, looking up at the endless blue sky and knew the emptiness of despair.

Ironically, José had risen above his depression. He seemed almost content on the island. He fished and cooked his catch with the islanders, laughed and teased with the native women. Then he would do his best to coax Dash to partake of the feast.

Dash had no appetite. What difference did it make if he ate or not? If he was already dead, he couldn't die of starvation, and if he was still alive, well, then perhaps he wished to die.

"Ah, here you are, Dashiell. You should have come with me. I explored the south end of the island—a very interesting place. You know, my friend, I'm worried about you." José sat down on the sand beside Dash, and his dark eyes showed his concern. "You seem to have lost hope, and without hope a man is nothing."

113

"So, I'm nothing. Just leave me be, José. I'm not good company."

José laughed. "Ah, but you are my only company, except for the natives, and I can't really talk to them. They cannot comprehend the life we left behind. Let us speak of those times, my friend. It will keep us sane. I'll go first. I come from a village in southern Spain—a beautiful village, high mountains, green fields. Always I wanted to go to sea, so at sixteen my father gave me permission to leave..."

21

The Best Of Friends

Thomas woke up with a start. The man called Shorty was back. His heavy boots made a dull thudding sound on the straw-covered floor. Shorty saddled one of the horses and rode out of the barn at high speed.

Thomas yawned. He was lost in that zone between waking and sleeping. There was something oddly familiar to him about the man riding off on horseback. It seemed like someone had just told him about a long horseback ride from a country village to a big city. The storyteller had captured Thomas's imagination with a vivid description of a crowded city teeming with street peddlers hawking their wares and horse-drawn carts that rumbled over cobblestones, contrasting sharply with elegant carriages adorned with gilt, from whose windows one could catch glimpses of beautiful, dark-eyed señoritas. The narrator had arrived at the waterfront where tall-masted ships had beckoned him aboard, beguiling him with the promise of adventure in far-away lands.

Thomas stretched. The memory was gone and sadly he saw that he was in a dirty cage and not lying on a sandy beach gazing at blue skies and listening to a fascinating story. *It must have been a dream,* he thought, *but whatever it was, it was certainly better than being here.* Thomas wished he could go back to sleep and reenter the dream world.

He couldn't see Hungry because their cages were side by side, but the two dogs were directly across from him, and he noticed the red Pekingese lay motionless on the floor of its cage. It had not stirred, neither when the man had passed, thumping his heavy boots, nor stranger still, when he had ridden past on that huge horse. The poodle had awakened and cringed in obvious terror when the man had entered. She barked now, three high-pitched little Yup-Yup-Yups.

The poor thing didn't even look real to Thomas, more like the toy dogs in store windows. She was stylishly clipped, with her tail ending in a little white pom-pom and on the top of her head was perched a tiny red satin bow. Thomas didn't completely understand what any of their roles were to be in the "pit fight," but that it would be gruesome, he had no doubt.

More footsteps, and this time it wasn't Shorty, but the other man who seemed to be a helper in the operation. "Chow time," he snorted.

When he came into view, Thomas could see that he had a large dish in his hand. The man opened the poodle's cage and again the dog shrank to the back. The man ladled something from the dish onto the floor of the cage. "Bet you're used to eatin off'a china," he said with a sneer. "That ole lady I snatched you from looked like one of them loonies what'a give a daug china plates. Now, eat that grub," he yelled, suddenly pulling the poodle's head down to the floor. She yelped pitifully, and the man laughed.

Next he opened the Pekingese' cage. "Wake up, ya lazy hound," he yelled, but the dog never moved. "Oh-Oh, Shorty ain't gonna like this. Dumb daug went and died on us." He pulled the dog's body out of the cage and tossed

116

it on the ground. "Shoot, ain't got time ta git another daug before the fight." He looked across to Thomas's and Hungry's cages. "You cats is in luck. One of ya gonna perform in the pit tonight."

Thomas hissed at him and when the man spooned the slop out of the dish into his cage, Thomas almost threw up from the smell of it. Before the man got to Hungry's cage, the older cat let out a yowl to wake the dead. Thomas couldn't imagine what was wrong.

"EEE-OW-EEE-OW-EEEECH," Hungry screamed in his powerful voice.

"You must be the wild one," the man said, and Hungry emitted an omnious low growl, which even raised the hairs on Thomas's back. "You jes go hungry. I ain't gonna git my hand bit. I'll tell Shorty he can git you outa the cage tonight. He knows so much 'bout handlin' animals, let him git his hand mauled. Never did like no cats nohow." Then he laughed. "Wait 'til tonight, wild cat. You'll warm up the doberman good fer the big fight."

Thomas saw it all clearly now. They were to be used as teasers before the main bout—a little something extra to whet the appretite of the vicious dogs for bigger prey, and a sadistic spectacle to arouse the crowd. Hungry had deliberately chosen to die first. "Why did you do that?" Thomas called out to his friend.

"I'd rather get it over with," Hungry answered calmly. "Besides, I've lived my life, such as it's been, and it ain't been much, Thomas. What do I have to look forward to? If we'd gotten to Florida, and you'd gone to live with the Bradfords, I'd just be roamin the streets again. I want you to know, though, that the best time of my life has been these weeks that we've been together."

"Don't give up, Hungry. Something might happen yet."

"You go on thinkin' that, Thomas. As for me, it's OK. Don't worry. I'm not scared or sad or anything, but there's one thing I'd like you to do for me in the time we've got left."

"What is it?"

"Tell me from the beginning all about them funny people ya stayed with, Marcy and Drew and that Pink Lady."

"Blue Lady," Thomas said softly.

"Yeah—The Blue Lady and Zorrie and the handsome son, Flash."

"Dash."

"Yeah. Tell me all about them, Thomas."

Thomas swallowed over the big lump in his throat and began. "Did I ever tell you about the time Sheba and I saved Marcy from a con-man? His name was Mr. Cottonwood and it was the funniest time ever...."

ତ୨   ତ୨   ତ୨

All day, Thomas told Hungry stories about those dear and crazy days with the Collins family. Even the poodle stopped her yapping and sat in the front of her cage, almost like she was listening, but of course that was impossible, because dogs can't understand the language of cats and vice versa.

Late in the afternoon, the man called Shorty came back. He yelled at the other man. "Git this daid daug outa here. Ya wanna stink up my whole barn?"

Then he stormed out, thumping the ground again with his heavy boots, and his helper rushed in, grabbed the

118

Pekingese's body and stuffed it into one of the discarded burlap bags. "Been workin like a daug all day, diggin' that pit," he grumbled, "while he's been ridin around takin bets. Ah ain't his slave."

Several hours later Thomas heard the sound of automobiles and motorcycles being driven onto the grounds. "Sounds like I'll be playin to a full house," Hungry quipped.

Helpless rage seized Thomas, and he screamed and threw himself against the walls of the cage in a futile effort to break out.

"Don't do that, Thomas," Hungry cried in a loud voice.

A line from Sir Percival's Revenge repeated itself in Thomas's head. *'Slay me if you will,' the king cried from the tower. 'But a king was I born, and a king will I die.'*

"I'm sorry, Hungry," Thomas said, his voice rational again. "I forgot myself. You're a brave cat, and when my time comes, I hope I can follow your example."

"I know you will, Thomas. One thing I want to say, though, before they come for me. Can I give you some advice?"

"Certainly, Hungry."

"If a miracle should happen and you should be spared, promise me you won't go to Florida. Promise me you'll go back to Marcy and Drew. I think that's where your heart lies, Thomas. I really do."

Thomas had no time to answer, for suddenly Shorty and the helper were striding into the barn. The helper went to the poodle's cage and pulled her out. The little dog was trembling all over, and even the ridiculous bow on the top of her head bobbed up and down in response.

Shorty went to Hungry's cage. "You're next, wild cat," he said, grabbing poor Hungry by the scuff of the neck and rendering him helpless. Hungry said not a word, and Thomas closed his eyes until the barn door banged shut.

22

Shipmates

The sun came up every morning and the moon came out every night, one day blending into another, and all of them exactly the same. It never rained, and yet the island was always green and bountiful. The temperature never varied, remaining always at a perfect degree, somewhere in the eighties—a gentle land, inhabited by a gentle people, who also never varied, as ageless as the time wherein they were trapped. Fearful that they had displeased the king, they left Dash alone to spend his time gazing out at the endless sea.

José would go off early in the morning and return late in the afternoon. Dash assumed he was amusing himself exploring the island. As for Dash, there was no amusement. He could not accept the present, felt he had no future and the past, for him, was a closed book.

José's daily wanderings down memory lane only served to fill Dash with lonely yearnings for himself and deep pity for José, whom he had learned to love as a brother. Dash yearned to return to the 20th century and José to the simpler world of 1650, two distinctly different desires. José relieved his homesickness by recounting incidents from his past to Dash, but Dash could not reciprocate, for to do so would shatter his friend's thin illusion of hope.

Every day Dash went to the beach and stretched himself out in the cool white sand to drink in the sun and listen to the waves gently lapping the shore. He lay now with his

eyes half-closed to the glare and noticed José coming toward
him. José waved and hurried forward.

"I have a surprise, my friend, one that will turn your
frown to a smile."

"You caught a fish," Dash said without interest.

"Something much better," José answered with all the
eagerness of a child.

At that moment, he reminded Dash of a childhood pal,
an eager, bright little lad in his Cub Scout troop.

"You caught a mermaid," Dash said, and smiled.

"Aha, you're getting better. I'd rather catch a mermaid
than a fish, but no, not a mermaid either. Come, let me
show you."

Dash yawned. "I'll take your word for it. Just tell me
about it."

"No. For three days you've sat on the beach, my friend,
doing absolutely nothing. Come on, you'll grow stiff and
turn into an old man on me." José playfully pounded Dash
on the arm. "Look at that muscle, soft as a woman's
already."

"Cut it out. I'm warning you," Dash said, but he couldn't
help laughing.

José danced around like a boxer, fists up, sparring with
a left and then a right, and soon Dash joined in, and the
two were wrestling like kids in the sand. They were close
to the water's edge and José swept his hand into the surf,
splashing water on Dash. "I can run like a rabbit," he said
with a laugh and sprinted down the beach with Dash in
pursuit.

José was a good runner, and Dash forgot his depression
in the chase. He laughed as José clowned ahead of him,

making remarkable strides, running in an exaggerated and comic gait. *If he'd been born in this century, he'd have been a comedian,* Dash thought. In spite of Dash's longer legs, José kept ahead, seemingly defying gravity, barely touching the ground and looking remarkably like a rabbit as he hopped in the air.

Suddenly José stopped, and Dash saw that they had come to the fern forest which opened out to the cove. Breathless, they faced each other. José's eyes glowed with excitement, but this time it was a boyish excitement, with no trace of the wild-eyed fear which had been present the first time he had lured Dash to this spot.

"Come, please, see my surprise," he said between gasps.

Dash nodded, and parting the giant fronds of ferns, they made their way to the cove and of course to the ship which lay waiting for José like a silent accomplice.

They swam the short distance to her and boarded her as before. This time though, José assumed the role of skipper rather than frantic deckhand.

Proudly he swept the ship with his eyes. "I've worked on her every day. She's sea-worthy now and ready to leave. We can make it, my friend. Are you with me?"

"You mean you'd sail out to sea on this ship again?"

"Yes, I would. Oh, I fear what may lie ahead, but I fear more spending the rest of my life on this island. I'm twenty-two years old, Dash, and you're twenty-one. We're two young men, and we deserve to live, to love, marry and beget children. I want to go home, and I'd rather die trying than give up and remain here, alive and yet dead."

"I don't know," Dash said. His head was whirling with thoughts. *Could this be done? Could they find their way*

123

back—back through whatever dimension they had passed to reach this state. Perhaps they could swing the same door open again. And then there was the gold.... The natives would let them take the gold. They'd already given it to them. At the price of gold today, Dash could be very rich. He could build a financial empire with that gold. But, what of José? What would happen to José if they crossed over into the twentieth century?

José was watching him closely and he said, "I'm going, my friend—with you or without you." Then he smiled and held out his hand. "Shipmates?"

"Shipmates," Dash said, clasping José's outstetched hand.

23

Almost Forgotten

"There's that dirty white cat again."

"Throw him a fish head."

"Here. Want this, Whitey?"

"Just throw it. He won't come to ya. That big cat been hangin' 'round this dock for nigh onto a year now. Won't come to nobody."

The young fisherman threw the fish head, and Thomas caught it in his mouth and took off. He ran under a pier and tore the raw fish apart with strong teeth. When he had finished, nothing was left but the scales and the eyes. Thomas looked at the dead eyes, discarded in the sand. They reminded him of something, but he deliberately refused to remember.

He was on the street again, but this time at least, Thomas ate well. There was no need to resort to rummaging in garbage cans or plotting elaborate schemes, or making friends with humans. This last, Thomas would not have done anyhow. He scrupulously avoided any contact with humans.

He had been surprised to hear the old fisherman say that he had been living on the dock for almost a year. Thomas had completely lost track of time. One day ended and another began, and his only concern was with eating and sleeping and keeping constantly on the alert against man, his enemy.

Thomas couldn't remember why man was his enemy, but he knew it was so with every fiber of his being. Sometimes at night he would awaken suddenly, his back fur bristling with fear, and he knew he had had the dream again. What the dream was, Thomas didn't know and didn't even want to know.

He was no coward; there wasn't a cat on the docks who'd tangle with him, nor a rat. Ordinarily dogs didn't bother him either, but once Thomas had seen a large and very sleekly built dog with dark, smooth hair, and a terrible thing had happened to Thomas that day. An icy chill had caused him to tremble violently, though the summer day was warm, and his feet had stuck to the pavement as if frozen into the cement. Thomas had not been able to move at all for several seconds, and then his stomach had flipped, and he had vomited right on the pavement, causing a shopkeeper to run screaming from his store and kick at him for defacing the sidewalk.

Thomas left the fish remains and walked briskly away from the wharf toward the center of town. He knew where he was going. There was a park in the heart of the downtown section, and being a loner, Thomas went there for his own amusement.

The park was overrun with squirrels, and it gave Thomas enormous pleasure to chase them. He'd never caught one and really didn't want to, for though they resembled mice facially, they were really nothing like those dirty little critters. They were industrious and frugal, burying their chestnuts and storing them for the winter famine, and their agility in the trees was something incredible to see. Thomas both admired and envied them their hair-raising flights from branch to branch with nary a misstep.

Would that I could be like the birds in the air, and the scurrying squirrels, who hop from tree to tree outside my window—free. But alas, this invisible crown holds me prisoner, far more cruel, my guard than thee.

The strange words were suddenly in Thomas's mind. He had no idea where he might have heard them. Often out of nowhere they came to him, these funny little quotes, like messages from a forgotten past.

Thomas retreated under an unoccupied bench to watch the squirrels. He had lost all desire to chase them and a vague depression had settled down over him. He was so alone and so lonely. Not a friend in the world did he, Thomas Bradford have, and lonelier still, not even the memory of a friend.

Thomas's sharp ears picked up the sound of approaching footsteps. Humans again! Was there no place on earth where they didn't intrude? He remained under the bench and watched their approach.

A man and woman walked toward him. The woman was small, almost child-like. She had a funny way of walking— slowly, but with a little skip in her step, and this drew Thomas's attention to her instead of to the man.

She had long, dark hair and she was dressed all in white—white slacks, white coat and a little white hat, which she had removed and held in her hand. They paused directly in front of Thomas's bench. He turned his attention to the man. Looking up, he saw only large tennis shoes and the bottoms of faded jeans. The bench creaked as they sat down on it.

The girl spoke. "I wish you'd forget it, Dave."

"That's been the problem, hasn't it?"

"Come on, Dave. You know what I mean. Dr. Jaspar's told you it'll all come back in time, if you'll let it."

"That's what worries me. Maybe I don't really want it to come back, Lisa. Maybe I won't let it."

"That's OK, too, Dave. The future's more important than the past, and your future can be anything you want it to be. Really, I get exasperated with you. Do you realize you *almost* died?"

The man laughed. "OK, OK. I get your point. I'll be patient and listen to my nurse, I promise."

"I'm not really a nurse yet, but *almost*," the girl said.

Again the man laughed. "You're the *almostest* girl I know. Let's see, you're *almost* a nurse, *almost* twenty-one, *almost* five feet tall..."

The girl laughed, too, but a strange feeling had overtaken Thomas. There was something familiar about the conversation, and even the man's voice seemed familiar. Thomas felt propelled by an unknown force. Trance-like, he walked out from under the bench and looked up into the face of the man.

"Look, a cat," the girl said. Both Thomas and the blond young man stared intently into each other's eyes. The girl looked from Thomas to the man. "What is it?"

"This odd-eyed white cat. There's something—I don't know," he stammered, obviously confused.

Thomas felt confused, too. What was it about this man?

"Here kitty, nice kitty," the girl said, extending her hand. Without thinking, Thomas allowed her to stroke him, and automatically a deep hum started in the back of his throat.

"Dave," the girl said softly. "Listen, he's purring. Let's take him back to your place and feed him. He's some kind of link, isn't he? Something triggered in your mind when you saw him. I know it did."

"I don't know," the man said vaguely, but the girl ignored him and continued stroking Thomas. Speaking in her soft voice, she said, "Nice kitty. Don't be afraid."

She picked Thomas up and cradled him in her arms. *She smells fresh and sweet, like flowers,* Thomas thought, and suddenly he felt very ashamed of his own appearance and the pungent order of fish which he knew clung to his fur.

Close to her now, Thomas saw that she was very beautiful with a small heart-shaped face and chestnut hair.

Chestnut hair, soft and full. Skin touched by the dew, but oh, her eyes—they mirrored a soul in which not one hint of unkindness grew.

Somehow Thomas knew the strange quotation applied explicitly to her, and all his apprehension vanished.

"See, Dave. He accepts our invitation to lunch. Come on," she said, pulling the man up with her free hand.

The man's basement flat was just around the corner from the park and once inside, Thomas saw that it consisted of three rooms and a bath—nothing fancy, but neat. Almost too neat. It was as if no vestige of the man himself was present in his living quarters.

The girl deposited Thomas on the floor and opened the refrigerator. She poured milk into a bowl and set it down on the floor, and Thomas eagerly lapped it up.

"Look at him, Dave. I'll bet he's never tasted milk before," the girl said.

But, Thomas knew this taste, and his mind conjured up a picture of a little old fat lady, although he didn't know what she had to do with him.

"I've never seen an odd-eyed cat before," the girl called Lisa said, and Thomas stopped lapping the milk and looked up at her.

She stood, leaning on the kitchen table in her white coat and white pants, and suddenly another picture flashed before Thomas's mind. It was of a man in a white coat and white pants. "He's going to be odd-eyed," the man had said.

The scene vanished as suddenly as it had appeared, and Thomas returned to his milk.

"He would be a beautiful cat if he were cared for," Lisa said. "Look at that fur. Why, if it was clean, it would look just like snow."

Thomas's busy tongue stopped in his gromming, and the man put down his cup and stared at Lisa.

"My mother had a cat named 'Snow,'" he said simply.

"Oh, Dave, you're starting to remember something."

"Not really," he added quickly.

"But, it's a start. I knew the cat meant something to you. This is just the beginning. More will come back. I know it will. Just try to remember."

Thomas was watching the man's face, and he saw a strange expression cross over it. "Isn't it about time for you to go on duty?"

Lisa looked worried. "I'll leave, Dave. Just don't close it off. Let it all come back and remember this. Nothing

130

will make any difference to me. I'm your friend, and I'll always be your friend."

"Don't commit yourself yet, Lisa. It may be bad luck to be my friend."

And mine as well, Thomas thought, as sudden memory took him back through time and space to an old barn, a lonely cage and the sound of...

24

Where The Heart Lies

"BRING ON THE DAUGS —BRING ON THE DAUGS."

They chanted it over and over, stomping their feet and clapping their hands till Thomas felt he would go mad. What were they doing? Where was Hungry? Maybe he had escaped, jumped right out of Shorty's arms and taken off, lickedy-split up a tree. Wouldn't that be something, old Hungry putting it over on them like that?

"Looka that lil piker run," someone shouted, and a roar went up from the crowd.

"Come on, Killer. What you waitin' fer?"

"He's got 'im now. Head 'im off. That's it."

The shouts died down and then there was silence.

"TEN MORE MINUTES TO PLACE BETS." That was Shorty's voice. "THE TIME WAS FOUR MINUTES AND TEN SECONDS FOR KILLER," he announced and the crowd roared its approval. "NEXT IN THE PIT'LL BE THE CHALLENGER, SATAN. THIS HERE DAUG'S A TENNESSEE CHAMPEEN. GONNA WARM 'IM UP WITH A WILD CAT."

Somebody shouted, "That ain't no wild cat, Shorty. Looks like a plain ole tom cat ta me."

Shouts drowned out the speaker, and Thomas flung himself at the door of the cage. He had to get out. He had to help Hungry, but a piercing whistle exploded in his ears. The shouts grew louder, and then a thunderous roar of stampeding feet drowned out the voices. Another piercing shriek from the whistle and then a voice, mighty in its intensity, yelled, "POLICE—THIS IS A RAID."

A few moments later, the barn door opened and a policeman walked in with Shorty. "What's in here?"

"Nothin'," Shorty answered. "I tole ya, ya got all the bets."

"What's in them cages?"

"Tigers."

"Wise guy, ain't ya."

The officer opened the cage, and Thomas ran out. He hid outside the barn and watched as the crowd of men were herded into paddy wagons.

When they had all gone, Thomas headed for the field. He spotted the poodle's body about a yard from the pit. Unrecognizable as a dog, she looked like a discarded wig tossed on a trash heap.

Thomas stood at the edge of the pit and looked down, forcing himself to scan every inch of the muddy hole, and then he jumped into it.

Warm blood still trickled from Hungry's torn throat and Thomas licked the wound. "This'll make it better, Hungry," he said as the dead eyes of his old friend stared up at him.

♋   ♋   ♋

The memory of it still hurt, but time, which was supposed to heal all wounds, had mercifully anestheized Thomas for almost a year. Now, he must look back and remember if Hungry's life was to have any meaning at all.

He left the man's apartment by way of the window and headed for the park. Thomas had much to think about.

However it be, it seems to me, tis only noble to be good. Kind hearts are more than coronets and simple faith more than royal blood.

That quotation, with apologies to Lord Tennyson, had been slightly altered by Marcy and appeared on the title page of *Sir Percival's Revenge.* The words haunted Thomas and filled him with regret. How foolish and self-important he had been, thinking himself a king, lording it over poor Hungry, whose simple goodness and noble courage he had overlooked until now, when it was too late.

And how had he repaid Marcy, whose kind heart far outweighed her accomplishments?

"I'll be leaving soon," old Sheba had said. "And they'll need you here."

Wrapped up in himself, he had scorned her for a foolish old cat, talking to hear herself talk, but now her words took on a new, ominous meaning.

What would Marcy do without Sheba? How would she write with no Sheba to sit on the desk and listen to the dictation? Who would give her comfort when the rejection slips arrived? And, what if another Mr. Cottonwood should try to work his designs on poor, unsuspecting Marcy?

Hungry's voice spoke to Thomas, "Go back, Thomas. I think it's where your heart lies. I really do."

25

The Final Curtain

She turned only once to wave. Then she hurried on toward the hospital across from the park. Dash watched her until she was out of sight, her small figure growing smaller and smaller, moving along in her funny little uneven gait.

He remembered the first time he had seen her. Heavily sedated, he had opened drugged eyes to see this apparition enter his room. The white hospital coat was too long for her short figure. It had reached to her ankles and with her face illuminated by the tiny flashlight she held, she had looked like a spirit to him.

"Are you an angel?" he had asked her.

"Almost," she'd whispered and smiled.

He had drifted off to sleep again, and in the morning, a heavy, middle-aged nurse had appeared, and he had forgotten his midnight visitor.

The next night she had appeared again, and in the morning Dash asked the day nurse about her. "That would be Lisa," she'd said. "She's a volunteer."

He had stopped taking the sleeping pill they gave him at night, determined to be awake when she came. More beautiful than he had imagined, she had a tremendous effect on Dash Collins, known at the hospital as David X. Her cheerfulness and courage would not let him give up.

Because she was crippled, she did not think of herself as attractive or desirable, but neither did she allow her handicap to depress her. All of her life she had wanted to be a nurse, but her disability was an obstacle.

Unable to pass the rigorous physical demanded by St. Mark's Hospital for admission to their nursing program, she had volunteered her services with the hope that her dedication and diligence would open the door. It hadn't, but undaunted, she had continued to fill in whenever and wherever needed.

Dash closed the door and returned to the apartment. The stray cat was gone, his paw prints on the window sill giving mute evidence of his escape route.

"Ungrateful devil," Dash muttered. "Drank your milk and took French leave." Lisa would be disappointed.

He sat in the large armchair and thought about his other life. He, too had been an ungrateful devil. How could he have turned his back on all the people who had loved him, especially in their time of need, simply because they couldn't give him what he wanted? Tears of shame and regret burned his eyes as he remembered the last time he'd seen his family. He had acted like a spoiled child.

All of it seemed so long ago, and the Dash Collins of those days seemed a stranger to him now. Somewhere along the line he had changed, grown up—but when and how? So much of it was still missing, clouded and shrouded in mystery.

He remembered traveling to Florida. Money had been the only thing on his mind. He was going to show his father he could be a success. He remembered going to Palm Beach and gaping at the limousines lining the streets. He'd own one someday, he'd told himself. He remembered a gambling casino in Miami and chips piled high in front of him. A great way to get rich quick, he'd thought, and then the chips had started to dwindle. The magic formula had ceased to work, and his luck had changed.

He remembered a bartender writing down a phone number for him. "The pay's good," he'd said. "The ship's not registered, you understand, something to do with taxes, but that shouldn't bother you."

It hadn't. He'd never even questioned it, nor why they'd hire on an inexperienced kid, nor most importantly, if the crates in the hold contained oranges and only oranges.

It would explain a lot of things—no ship reported missing, and yet he'd been picked up floating half-dead in a life raft. What a fool he had been!

Lisa called during her supper break. Dash told her nothing, and he knew she was disappointed and a little hurt that he wouldn't confide in her, but he couldn't help himself. How could he tell Lisa that the man he was discovering was hardly a man at all—more a spoiled, indulgent child? How could he justify himself in her eyes when he couldn't even bear to part the final curtain and face himself? And that was the crux of the matter. There was more, much more that he couldn't remember. Why?

Something had happened to him after abandoning the ship—something so painful that he had blotted it out and until he knew what that something was, he could not come to terms with himself. He could neither go back and face his family, nor could he go forward and face the future, until he remembered. So he forced himself to remember....

26

The Other Side Of Time

The day they left the island, he stood on the shore and watched the natives load the casks on board. He remembered thinking how ironic it seemed that they would want to leave this island paradise where the sun always shone, where gentle breezes caressed the shore, where food and drink were always plentiful and there was no death—to chart a course into the unknown, facing untold hardships, risking their very lives, and in the end, for what? To return to an imperfect world?

But, when the ship was ready, he had hurried aboard, eager to be off, and he had raised a clenched fist to José, his comrade in adventure.

"Did you notice?" José asked. "I changed the ships's name to *Consuela. Marguerita* is bad luck, so I didn't think you'd mind. Consuela is a girl in my village."

"Consuela is a fine name," Dash said. He hadn't cared what the ship was called. *Just let it get us through the time warp—and make me a millionaire,* he'd added as an afterthought.

José hadn't wanted to take the gold. "Maybe it was bad luck for us. It was blood money anyway. Spain makes slaves of the Indians in Mexico and now she steals their gold."

But Dash had insisted.

"The king will confiscate it," José warned.

Dash gave him no answer. How could he explain to José that his much feared king was a handful of ashes on the other side of time. *If we make it,* he remembered thinking, *we'll be rich, and José will adjust to a new life.*

And so they had sailed on a beautiful morning of blue skies and calm seas. Watching the island fade in the distance, they had grown silent, each locked in his own thoughts.

José had spoken first. "You're a strange man, my friend."

"In what way?"

"Not once have you spoken to me of your life before coming to the island."

Dash wrestled with his conscience. What was he to do? The whole thing was so bizarre, it defied a rational explanation, and moreover, José was an uneducated man, born in an era when science was in its infancy. If he told him the truth, he would never believe him, and so he lied. He concocted a tale which would have done his mother proud. Falling back on his high school history, he had woven a story of an indentured servant who had escaped and gone to sea.

The story completely satisfied José. "Have no fear, good friend. You shall come to Spain with me. They'll never find you there."

José's warm sympathy had touched Dash. Centuries removed in time and space, and yet he felt he could count this man his greatest friend. Their's was a unique companionship, one in which they seemed to compliment each other.

Dash, who was conscious of the supernatural aspect of their voyage, had misgivings and moments of fear, while José, ignorant of the true facts, never wavered in his optimism.

On the fifth day out, Dash noticed a change. The sky was just as blue, and the sea just as calm, but they felt a pull at the stern, as if unseen hands were drawing them back. All that day they had felt it—one knot forward, and then one knot back. José, the experienced sailor, was at a loss to understand it, and Dash started to worry.

That night while José slept and Dash held watch, a strange thing happened: The stars suddenly disappeared, as if a curtain had been drawn in the sky, and a strong wind arose, catching the sails and propelling the vessel forward at such speed that Dash was thrown to the deck. It felt as if the ship had taken wings, and crawling on his hands and knees, Dash made his way below deck.

José was awake, but he looked strange, different. "Are you sick?" Dash asked.

"Madre Dios—Madre Dios."

It was the first time Dash had heard José speak Spanish and the words had chilled him with their implications. The ship lurched then and they both fell. The pull had been uncanny—those powerful underwater hands, pulling them back, as the strong wind fought to pull them forward.

With superhuman strength, Dash raised himself up. "I won't go back. I won't go back," he shouted.

The lifeboat, he thought. Thank God he had insisted on bringing the lifeboat on board. "José," he shouted over the wind. "We're abandoning ship. Get to the lifeboat, José.

This ship is being forced back through time again. José, José."

He had crawled to the other side of the cabin where José lay fallen.

"We must hurry," he said, grabbing José's arm. His fingers closed on shriveled flesh instead of hard young muscle. "José," he screamed, looking into the face of a wizened old man. The ancient skin was paper thin, and it began to disintegrate before his eyes, exposing the skeletal bones underneath. He dropped his grip on José's arm and ran from the sight of his lifeless body.

Once on deck, he'd fought his way toward the lifeboat, untied it and heaved it overboard into the churning sea. An uncarthly blue lightening flashed across the black sky and he'd jumped free of the ship as another gigantic pull forced her backwards, splintering the main mast and sending it crashing into the sea.

Remembering those events hurt, and Dash Collins wept without shame. Reliving that fateful night had been necessary, though. Now he knew why he had buried the past and he asked himself the question he had been unable to face: Had he known, deep within himself, from the very beginning, José's ultimate fate? And had the gold been a factor in his decision to keep José in the dark?

Who can say? he answered himself.

"I'm leaving, with you or without you," José had said, and he had meant it. Would it have mattered to this headstrong and eager-to-live youth if Dash had told him death waited on the other side? Probably not, and yet, Dash wished with all his heart that he had left the gold on the island. Only then could he be certain beyond a shadow of a doubt.

141

José's eager young face flashed into his mind. Home and family had been very important to José. A good friend, was he, even now, trying to tell Dash something?

CHAPTER

27

Home At Last

A light snow was falling, and it dressed the woods in shimmering glory. The country air was fresh and he inhaled deeply, remembering the unique and wonderful aroma of spruce and pine. He paused to drink in the beauty of it all, and then he hurried, for his long journey was finally at an end. Thomas Bradford was coming home.

He dashed through the woods, a ghostly little figure, white on white against the swirling flakes. He stopped short when he saw the house. It looked the same, and he asked only that it be the same.

A light went on in the kitchen, casting a glow on the snow-covered lawn. *That would be Marcy, fixing supper,* he thought. In the morning, she would come to the door and throw out crumbs for the birds, and Sheba would watch from the window. Or would she? It had been almost two years. Two years was a long time to an old cat like Sheba.

Should he wait until morning? Drew might come out soon to use the incinerator. Would Drew know him? Or, would he think him a stranger—a feral cat? Stray kittens were taken in and given homes, but not grown cats. People figured grown cats could fend for themselves. Hungry had known that.

"You see, Thomas, cats have to find homes when they're young. When I was a kitten, I was afraid of people, so I never found no home, and now its too late. Nobody wants no growed cat!"

Thomas swallowed hard. Maybe it was too late for him, too. He wanted to see them, though. If they didn't want him, well, that would be his bad luck.

He shattered the stillness of the night with a yowl that sent a mouse scurrying for safety. The porch light went on, and the door burst open. For a split second, there was dead silence, and then Marcy screamed, "Drew, come quick. It's Snowbaby. He's come home. Oh, I can't believe it. Look at him. Look how big he is. Oh, Snow, what a Christmas gift you are."

They brought him inside and Marcy brushed the snow from his coat with a towel.

Drew said, "Marcy, are you sure he's the same cat? This is hard to believe."

Marcy was sitting on the floor, and she stopped rubbing Thomas and looked up at her husband with a startled expression on her face. "Drew, I can't believe you don't recognize him. Of course, it's Snowbaby. Look at his face. Look at his eyes." She waited. "Well, I just KNOW it's him," she said with finality, slightly impatient that Drew should question anything so obvious.

Drew was a good man, but a practical one, Thomas knew. The poor soul couldn't help his lack of intuition, so Thomas supposed he'd have to convince him.

He sauntered into the dining room and leaped to the top of the buffet, his favorite old hiding place.

"There. You see that." Marcy smiled with satisfaction. "Remember how he used to hide there when he was little, and we'd look all over the house for him?"

144

Drew looked up and Thomas peered down. "Well, I'll be darned," he said. "Where in the world do you suppose he's been all this time?"

Marcy winked an eye at Thomas. "Leading his secret life, I suppose."

Thomas jumped down and just to show Drew there were no hard feelings, he rubbed up against Drew's pants legs and purred for him. "Well, I'll be darned," Drew said again, stroking Thomas under the chin.

Thomas sniffed the air, but the scent of Sheba was no longer in the house. He had expected as much, but the knowledge saddened him nevertheless. It would have been nice if Thomas could have made his peace with old Sheba.

Marcy, who had the keenest intuition of any human Thomas had ever known said, "You're looking for Sheba, aren't you, Snow? Sheba's gone. Poor old girl caught pneumonia the very night you and Dash left home. Winston did his best, but he couldn't save her."

The front door opened, and Zorrie, her arms laden with packages, came in. "Merry Christmas," she sang in her lilting voice. Dumping the packages on the sofa, she rubbed her arms. "It's getting cold, but it's so beautiful—a white Christmas. Oh, I love it." She took a breath. "Dash here yet?"

"Not yet. Oh, your face is cold," Marcy said, kissing Zorrie's cheek.

"Where's Grandmom and Winston?"

"They'll be over soon. They just got in today."

"The Honeymooners," Zorrie said, rolling her eyes. "How was Hollywood. Did they say?"

"They'll tell you all about it. Or, should I say your grandmother will tell you. Poor Winston probably won't get a word in."

Thomas was surprised. *The Blue Lady and Doc Winston going on a honeymoon. They had to be every bit of ten cat years old,* he thought.

"Zorrie, you haven't noticed our surprise visitor," Marcy said.

"It's Snow," Zorrie cried, spotting Thomas on the window sill. "Where did he come from?"

"Well, I'll be," her father said. "You mean you can tell right off that cat is Snow."

"Of course," Marcy answered impatiently, and then she turned to Zorrie. "He appeared at the kitchen door not fifteen minutes ago. Look how he's grown. Your father didn't believe he was our Snow, but he jumped right up on the buffet."

"His favorite spot." Zorrie smiled, and she patted Thomas on the head. "Oh, Snow, how nice. You and Dash both home for Christmas. Isn't that ironic? They left the same day, and they come home the same day." Cupping Thomas's face in her hands, she gazed into his unfathomable eyes. "Did you have a secret life somewhere else?" Then turning to her mother, she said, "Speaking of secret lives, did you tell Dash about the book?"

"No, I thought I'd surprise him."

Here we go again, Thomas thought. *Probably another crook is trying to take Marcy in with fat promises. I won't let anything happen,* he mentally promised old Sheba.

Marcy grew serious and looking at Zorrie, she said, "Zor, did Dash tell you anything?"

"No, Mom, honestly. It was the same as what he told you and Dad. He'll explain when he sees us. He sounds wonderful, and he loves us. That's the most important thing."

"Yes, that's all that matters," Marcy said.

"Not completely," Drew added. "He owes us an explanation."

"Drew, please don't," Marcy pleaded, but Drew gave her no answer.

Zorrie smiled at her mother and said in an undertone, "It'll be OK, Mom. I just know it will."

28

Family Reunion

"And that's the story," Dash said. "I know it's crazy, and fantastic, like something out of an old Jules Verne book. I won't feel hurt if you don't believe me. Nobody else has, except Lisa." He glanced in her direction and smiled. "I couldn't tell you anything about this before because I've been grilled in secret by the army, the navy, the FBI and the CIA, and they've all decided I'm nuts, but harmless."

Drew spoke first. "Son, could it have been a very vivid dream, either during your hospital stay, or while you were unconscious in the lifeboat, drifting for all those days? Now, I don't mean to disparage your story..."

"Dad. It's OK. You don't have to apologize. I respect your opinion."

Marcy glanced quickly at Zorrie. *Was this Dash, the stubborn hothead talking?*

He has changed, Marcy thought, her eyes softening as she looked at her handsome son.

"I thought of that, too, Dad. And there's only one thing wrong—the time element. I hired on the yacht May 15, 1999. I was found, unconscious, drifting in a lifeboat by the Coast Guard on May 30, 2000—over a year later." He put up his hand. "Wait, I know what you're going to say—that I signed on May 15, 2000, not 1999. Well, I can't prove it, but I know it was 1999, one month after I left home. If I'm wrong, then the year in between is a blank to me.

"The CIA thought I was lying about the time, and they ran an extensive check on my activities between April of 1999 when I arrived in Florida and when I was picked up at sea, but it was as though I had dropped off the earth. I believe that is exactly what happened."

The Blue Lady spoke at last. She had been silent for all of fifteen minutes. Thomas was sure it was a record for her and a tribute to Dash's spellbinding story.

"I've always believed in UFO's and those little space people, and to think my own grandson... Why it should be the subject for your mother's next book—a true account."

"Hold on, Grandmom. What I've said is strictly confidential. I don't want it to leave this room." He looked at his mother. "Sorry Mom, but I don't want to exploit this. Enough people already think me some kind of a nut. Besides," he said with no trace of sarcasm, "I want to see you get *Sir Percival* published."

"Oh, your mother has..." The Blue Lady stopped abruptly, as Marcy flashed her a warning look. "Your mother has a surprise for you," she finished lamely.

Dash had other things on his mind though, and he ignored the comment. "There is something else I want to say." Taking his whole family in with a glance, he continued. "I was a jerk. I acted like a spoiled brat, and I hope you'll all forgive me."

They started to protest, but he held up his hand. "It's true. However, they say there's something of value to be gleaned from even the worst experience, and I know one thing—my values have really changed."

149

Thomas listened and agreed. *Kind hearts and coronets,* he thought, *but kind hearts are best.*

"Now," Dash said. "Let me hear about all of you." He turned to Lisa and smiled. "My family's not like me. They're all exceptional people."

Lisa smiled back, a beautiful smile, and Marcy's intuition told her a secret that warmed her heart.

The Blue Lady said, "Your mother's..."

But Marcy interrupted her again. "Tell him about the wedding, Mother."

"Whose wedding?" he asked.

"Your grandmother and I were married last month," Winston said proudly.

"Hey, that's great. I had no idea." Dash shook hands with Winston and hugged his grandmother.

"We just got back from our honeymoon," The Blue Lady said.

"We went to Hollywood," Winston added and Thomas thought he had never seen Winston so animated. "Buela took the town by storm."

"Oh Winston, stop." The Blue Lady giggled and blushed.

"It's true." Winston said and then turned back to Dash. "Your grandmother knew so many people, and they all remembered her."

"Only one," The Blue Lady admitted, but she looked as pleased about it as Winston. "Matt Lewis is a big man at Disney Studios now, but when I knew him, he was a song and dance man. I mentioned to him about..." She looked askance at Marcy. "Well, aren't you ever going to tell him?"

150

"Tell me what?" Dash asked.

Marcy handed him a book, and Dash turned it over and looked at the cover. "Wow, Mom. You did it. You really did it."

"Isn't it wonderful?" Zorrie cried.

All of them gathered around Dash and were looking at the book he held in his hands. Thomas got up from the hearth and squeezed in between Winston and the Blue Lady for a peek. He could hardly believe his own eyes. On the front was a full-color, blown up picture of Thomas himself. And above the picture in bold letters, he read, *The Secret Life Of Thomas Bradford.*

"See—See your picture, Snowbaby?" the Blue Lady crooned.

"Dear, they can't distinguish pictures," Winston said.

Dash leafed through the book. "This is wonderful. Hey, Lisa. My mother's an author. What do you think of that?"

"A published author," Marcy added. "And I owe it all to Sheba and Snowbaby."

She hugged Thomas and pulled him on her lap. "And I thought I'd lost him forever."

"But, how did this come about?" Dash asked.

Thomas was anxious to hear this, too, so he settled down on Marcy's lap and listened intently as she spoke:

"Well, like I told you, Sheba died shortly after you and Snow left. I couldn't write anymore. I was worried about you and Snow, and I missed Sheba so much. One day I was sitting in my office, just thinking to myself about all those reams of paper I had wasted on the Sir Percival novels. Nobody was ever going to publish them, I told myself, and suddenly I just snapped. I became furious at the unfairness of it all, and I threw *Sir Percival's Revenge* across the room, and then I walked over and stomped on it."

Dash laughed. "Mom, I can't imagine you doing that."

"Of course you can't. I never made a spectacle of myself before any of you. Only Sheba and Snow were treated to my temper tantrums."

How true, Thomas thought, licking Marcy on the hand to show her he understood.

"Anyway, after I got it all out of my system, I became very calm, and I found myself moving over to the desk and sitting down. I almost expected to see Sheba sitting there waiting for me to begin. I turned on the tape recorder and started to dictate, *The Secret Life of Thomas Bradford.* Don't ask me where it came from because I really don't know." Marcy smiled. "It could even be true. Only Snow knows for sure, and he's not talking. Are you Snow?"

They all looked at Thomas, and he regarded them with a cat's mysterious, unfathomable eyes.

29

A Heart's Greatest Need

It was a white Christmas. Thomas sat in the window and peered at snow covered fields. He watched the sun rise and spread its light all over the countryside. It was so good to be home.

He heard someone tiptoe down the stairs, and he turned and saw it was Zorrie. She came to the window and looked outside, too. "A beautiful white Christmas," she said, and rubbed Thomas behind his ear.

"You ALWAYS had to be first on Christmas morning."

Zorrie and Thomas both turned at the sound. It was Dash.

Zorrie smiled. "Remember how mad you used to get when you'd sneak downstairs and I'd already be here?"

"Of course. I wanted to be first."

"It's so good to have you home, Dash. We all missed you."

"Me, too."

"Are you going back to Harvard? You can, you know. The book's already a success."

He answered her with a question. "What's Dad been doing?"

"He was working as a consultant from home. They were managing, but when Mom finished the book, he took over

153

as her agent. He took off for New York with the manuscript and wound up getting three top publishers to bid on it. Now that it's published, he's lined up a promotional tour."

"No kidding. You mean signing autographs and stuff?"

"The works, radio and TV appearances. They're booked in about twenty or more cities around the country. They'll be gone for months."

"What about the cat?"

"Snow? Oh, I suppose Grandmom and Winston will take care of him."

"I'd like to take him with us."

"What do you mean?"

"I'm going back to North Carolina, Zorrie. I've already registered in school there, and I have a job at night. It's time I stood on my own feet. I'm going to study oceanography. I have some theories of my own, and I'm in love with Lisa."

Zorrie smile indulgently. "Who'd have guessed."

"She's a wonderful girl, Zor. She's like you and Mom—kindhearted, and she's had such a rough time."

"What was it, Dash—polio?"

"No. She was born that way. Her father couldn't accept it, and he walked out on Lisa and her mother the day she was born."

"Oh, no."

"It's been his loss. According to her mother, he was a real jerk, a perfect specimen, or so he thought. He couldn't take it that a child of his was flawed—almost, but not quite, perfect. He had some money, and he set up a trust fund for Lisa. After twenty years, it's no fortune, but she manages. Her mother died three years ago, and Lisa came

154

to North Carolina. She's always wanted to be a nurse, but they wouldn't accept her because of the handicap. So, she works as a volunteer.

"One of the doctors at the hospital is interested in her case—wants to operate. Lisa wants it, too. It won't be easy. She'll be in a cast for months, but she wants to go through with it. She wants to be a nurse and do some other things in life she's missed, like getting all dressed up in high heels and going dancing. To me, she perfect right now, but I want what she wants. Anyway, back to the cat—Lisa loves cats and she's convinced that Snow's the same cat we saw in North Carolina, the one that brought my memory back. I think it would help her if she had him around."

They both looked at Thomas and he turned and stared out the window, deep in thought. He saw himself a cocky, half-grown cat, standing under the willow tree on a spring night.

"I'll be leaving and they'll need you here," old Sheba said, but Thomas had walked away.

This time he wouldn't walk away, for as the king said to Sir Percival in the closing chapter of *Sir Percival's Revenge:*

No more a king—no more a fool,

This be my creed,

A heart's greatest need,

Is the need to be needed.

THE END